Firestarter

Published by Jan Stryvant

Cover Credits: eBook Launch
(http://ebooklaunch.com/)

ISBN: 9781081150112

#62953

Jan Stryvant Books:

The Valens Legacy:

Black Friday	Book 1
Perfect Strangers	Book 2
Over Our Heads	Book 3
Head Down	Book 4
When It Falls	Book 5
Stand On It	Book 6
Vegas Rules	Book 7
Desperate Measures	Book 8
Secret Treaties	Book 9
It Ain't Easy	Book 10
Red Skies	Book 11
Demon Days	Book 12
Simple Things	Book 13
Trying Times	Book 14
Firestarter	Book 15

Shadow

Day by Day

"You called, Sean?" Oak asked as he came into Sean's workshop.

Sean looked up from his workbench, which had Estrella's necklace sitting on it. He'd borrowed it from her this morning to see if he could figure out how to copy the invisibility function on it, so he could work it into all of his wives' necklaces, or perhaps make them new ones. So far it wasn't going as easily as he would have liked. Repairing it had been a lot easier than copying.

"Yeah, I need you to pack those up for shipment," Sean said, motioning at the machines against the wall. The last week he'd been doing nothing but working on getting those built; they had a shortage of collars, silver tags, and even medallions in Europe. The First wanted to see if humans wearing one of his mind spell-negating medallions might be protected from having their souls ripped out and their minds possessed, so Sean had built one of those as well.

"You're building machines again?"

"Just those four, I finished the last one this morning. Right now I'm working on something new," Sean said, motioning to the materials on his workbench. "Sometime tomorrow a couple of lions are going to show up to pick those up, which is why I need them packed and read to go."

"Where are they going?"

"Europe, if I had to guess." Sean set his notes down and looked up at Oak. "How's everything holding together? I haven't really had the chance to sit down and talk with you in a while, Oak. Got anything you need?"

"Oh, things are fine, Sean. If I need anything, mostly I just ask Roxy or Daelyn."

Sean grinned. "Anything you need that they won't give you, then?"

Oak laughed. "If I thought they'd say no, I'd have come to you first. Last thing I need is for them to see me going over their heads."

"If you have to go over their heads, I'm the one who's going to be asking questions, so I wouldn't worry about them. How's Minnie doing? And what's everyone saying when I'm not around?"

"Minnie's doing good. She delivered twins last week."

Sean sighed. "And now I feel like a total heel. I totally forgot she was due. Sorry about that."

"We know you've been busy, Sean."

"Still, bring them by one of these nights for dinner so we can all see 'em. If the girls haven't seen them, I'm sure they'll feel guilty."

"And if they have?"

Sean grinned evilly. "Then *I'll* make them feel guilty for not reminding me! So what's the story on everyone else? Anything going on with the troops out there that they won't tell me about?"

"Well, have you been following the news at all?"

Sean grimaced. "I've been trying to avoid it."

"It's been getting pretty bad. Not the news so much right now, but there's been a lot of stories floating around trying to push anti-lycan sentiment, as well as anti-lion stories."

"I'm sure it'll blow over, Oak."

Oak shook his head. "I think you should call your friend Steve."

Sean thought about that. "Are our people getting that upset about it?"

"Up here? No. But I was talking to some of Art's wolves down in Sacramento, the ones helping to set up better security at the Sapientia council there, and they've been hearing some ugly comments when they're out in public."

Sean blinked. "People are getting in their faces?"

"Not yet. But you know how mundanes underestimate our hearing. They've been hearing more than a few muttered insults."

Standing up, Sean swept his work into the top drawer of his workbench and locked it with a simple spell.

"Guess I need to call Steve. If you could get those taken care of?"

"I'll get someone right on it."

"And don't forget to bring Minnie and the kids by."

"Wouldn't miss it," Oak said with a grin.

Walking outside, Sean got out his phone, checked his messages, and then dialed Steve.

"So, calling about all the bad press, I take it?"

"What, no 'hello Sean, how are you today?'" Sean teased.

"Right now I'm thinking I should have gotten on the plane with you and flew back to Reno," Steve said with a heavy sigh. "The president's still on our side; same for all of the important government agencies, and more than a few of the folks in Congress. As I understand it, secret briefings have been going on with a lot of the pols, bringing them up to speed on what happened in the embassy, as well as what happened on the highway."

"I hear a 'but' in there," Sean said.

"Yup. They know you pretty much executed all the people who attacked you on the highway, that you didn't accept surrender. It's being kept quiet, but there are some folks right now who aren't very pleased with you."

"Why do they think that? Do they have pictures?"

"No, thank god, but the forensics are supposed to be clear enough that they've drawn a few conclusions. I think some folks have bought my explanation that we rounded up all the weapons before we left, and the people who were shot lying down were still engaging us.

"But I'm not so sure everyone is buying it."

"Well, I guess that explains some of the supply issues I've been hearing about. At least it's nothing more than annoying right now," Sean replied, "but I heard there's something else going on?"

"Yeah, someone with a lot of money has taken out a pretty substantial PR campaign against us."

"Who?"

"Who do you think?"

"The German government?"

"Bingo."

"Well, I guess their request for our help really was just a ruse then."

"I've been trying to get some of the local reporters to pick that story up, but no takers so far."

"They afraid?"

"More like they're too stupid to recognize propaganda when they see it," Steve said with a sigh.

"Well, what about running our own propaganda?"

"We're working on it, but right now all the ALS people seem to be in town, and going around isn't always safe. Our people out here are being engaged damn near every day now. They're really spoiling for a fight, trying to provoke us."

"Maybe you *should* think about coming home, Steve."

"I don't know, Sean. That just feels like running away to me."

"If you can't accomplish anything, what's the point of being there? And more importantly, Steve, I can't afford to lose another friend."

Sean waited as Steve digested that for a minute.

"I don't think it's that bad here yet," Steve finally replied. "But trust me; I've got Terri and Tisha here to worry about. Not to mention the hundred some odd people working for me. If it gets any worse, of if any of our security people start getting worried, we'll leave."

"Don't be afraid to ask for more people, either," Sean said. "You might also want to see about moving to a new location."

"The problem with that is I'm pretty sure the spies Germany has here will out us."

"Talk to Duncan, see what he's got available."

"Why would he have anything? Hell, why would he even want to help?"

"Well, I can think of three reasons right off the top of my head. First, he's probably still got a lot of open lycan quarters from before they freed theirs, even if they never kept a lot. Second, we're allies. That works both ways."

"And third?"

"If things are heating up in DC, he just might appreciate the extra bodies to help protect him and his as well." Sean paused a moment. Thinking about that triggered a few thoughts. "You know what, call him, and call Eruditio, too. I'm gonna have Oak send out another hundred troops, maybe more. See if you can't get permission to billet some of our people on their grounds no matter what you end up doing. It'll spread 'em out so they're less likely to be noticed, and if Sapientia or Eruditio do become targets there, we won't have to scramble to help them out."

"You think they will?"

"Eruditio *did* take down the Vestibulum's high council."

"You think the Vestibulum…?"

"No, I think the djevels and maybe some of their allies might now see the mages as a threat and decide to go after them preemptively."

"What about the Ascendance and the Vestibulum? Want me to call them?"

"If they want it, they can call us and beg," Sean growled. "Well, maybe not the Ascendance, they at least came around. But I think it'll be a very cold day before we help the Vestis."

"Got it."

"Anything I can do to help with the PR?"

"Actually," Steve chuckled over the phone, "if you're gonna send me that many bodies, I have an idea for a nice little guerrilla marketing campaign. The big problem was, I couldn't do that and still swing security with all the ALS asshats in town."

"Well, whatever you do, understand you need to do it *everywhere*. This thing has spread beyond the beltway; we need to start getting ahead of it."

"What's my budget?"

"I'll talk to Deidre, but I don't think we can afford to cheap out on this one, Steve. If we lose public support, we could lose the war as well."

"Okay, I'm on it."

"Bye," Sean said and hung up. Looking up, he saw Oak coming back with the crew to pack up the machines.

"Oak," Sean called, walking over to him.

"Talk to Steve?"

"Yeah, we're sending him another two hundred. I want people who are well trained in small unit tactics and who understand how to keep things on the down-low and out of sight. They may end up bunking on the grounds of one of the councils, so make sure there isn't anyone with a grudge."

"You want me to send them with weapons?"

Sean nodded. "Armor, too."

"That means we'll have to charter an airplane."

"I know. Make it happen. Don't be surprised if you get some strange requests from Steve or Granite, either."

Oak laughed. "I'm *never* surprised when I get a strange request from anyone working for Steve anymore!"

"Thanks, Oak," Sean said and, stretching, he decided that now was as good a time as any to get some lunch before he went back to work on Estrella's necklace. He wondered idly if perhaps his uncle Maitland could find the original maker for him? Fey did live a very long time.

Sean dropped into one of the seats at a table in the main mess. He didn't eat here often, actually he hadn't eaten in the main mess since he'd come back, as this building hadn't been built yet. With all the troops here now, they'd had to put together something larger than what they'd been using.

But again, as the boss, he didn't eat with the grunts very often, because nobody wanted their boss looking over their shoulder all the time. But every once in a while it was appreciated. He was a lot more to them than just their boss, after all.

"Hey! Slumming with the rest of us?" asked Frank, one of the werewolves from Hunter's team, setting his tray down and dropping into one of the seats next to Sean.

"Yeah, just longing for the good 'ole days when we were in that building downtown and we'd all eat together every morning." Sean sighed.

"I hear it's all fixed up again."

"Yeah, I went by there a couple weeks ago to check on Alex after he got shot. It looks nice, but I really didn't have the time to check it out when I was there."

"Ah, I see the Pride of the Marines is here," Frank said, nodding over towards the chow line.

"Huh?" Sean said, looking over. There were a group of Marines in fatigues, looking as sharp as always. Sean often wondered how they did it. With them was a very attractive young woman. He searched his memory a moment, and then recalled her name, Betty.

"That gal with 'em. She's like their property," Frank said with a chuckle. "Regular party girl, I guess you'd say."

Sean blinked and remembered where Betty had come from and what she'd looked like. Straight-laced was almost an understatement; the way she'd looked and acted when Stewart had brought her by had made it clear she'd led something of a sheltered life. Nothing like the young and very daringly dressed young woman he was looking at now.

"Her?" he asked.

Frank laughed. "I know, right? And since she's latched on to the Marines, well, word is they'll thump you one if you go putting the moves on her."

Sean watched her as she went through the food line with the Marines around her. There were a lot of little 'public displays of affection' floating around between her and the men. She definitely seemed a lot more at ease.

When they finished getting their food, Sean raised his hand and waved them over as they started looking for a place to sit.

"Sure you wanna do that, Boss?"

Sean snorted. "Just want to be sure she's happy."

Sean watched as they all trooped over and, taking a good look at him, they took up all of the remaining seats at the table. Betty was giving him a little bit of that 'deer in the headlights' look as she whispered something to the man she was with. As a group they were all big guys, ranging from probably five and a half feet tall to over six feet. Each of them was built pretty impressively.

They were definitely built a lot heavier than most of Sean's wolves, and pretty much all the men in the infantry they'd picked up.

"Guys," Sean said smiling at all of them. "Take a load off. Don't believe I've had the pleasure to meet any of you yet. I want to thank you all for signing on; my commanders have been very happy to have the Marines onboard."

One of the older-looking men, whose rank insignia pinned to his collar had rockers under the bar, replied.

"Thank you, Sir. I don't believe we've been formally introduced."

Sean nodded. "You'll excuse me if I'm not familiar with your rank insignia there, Sergeant…?"

"Gunnery Sergeant Wyatt."

"Ah, right. Sean Valens. I'm the lion in charge of all this, and of course all of you as well." Sean leaned forward a little bit and lowered his voice, he didn't believe for a minute they didn't already know who he was. "And if you think generals can get cute when you start playing games with them, trust me when I say, us lions got them all beat.

"So, how do you like being a jag?" Sean continued, sitting back up.

Wyatt blinked and looked at Sean in surprise, while Frank just rolled his eyes.

"I like it. I like it a lot. I'm a lot stronger now, and I'm definitely tougher."

Sean looked around the table. "Are you all jags? Kind of hard to tell from here."

"Lance Troy and Corporals Moss and Lee are tigers. Same for Sergeant Dall over there. Corporals Ulrich, Rice, and Sergeant Masters are bears."

"How many of you have your hybrid forms down?"

Sean noticed only two hands went up.

"That's pretty good; you guys were infected what, three weeks ago?"

"Four, actually," Wyatt said, looking a little uncomfortable. Sean got the feeling he'd touched on a sore spot.

Sean nodded and went back to eating his breakfast. "Try spending more time in your animal form, as much as you can. It helps."

Glancing down the table, Sean saw that Betty was still looking a little nervous.

"Nice to see you again, Betty. You're definitely looking a lot better since Stewart brought you by. Everything going okay?"

"Ummm, well…" Betty blushed, looking down at her plate.

"I'm hoping that means 'yes'," Sean said with a smile. "Still thinking of getting infected?"

Betty's head came up and she looked at him, surprised. "Maybe?" she squeaked in a small voice.

"Stop picking on Betty," the guy sitting next to Wyatt said.

"You are?" Sean asked looking at him curiously.

"Corporal Lee," the man said with a warning look.

Sean nodded and held up a finger to him, then turned back to Betty. "Be sure to talk to some of the more experienced lycans before you make up your mind. I'll be sure to give permission to whomever you ask."

"Permission? She doesn't need your permission!" Corporal Lee said.

Sean noticed that the people sitting behind Lee were getting up and quickly moving away. Frank was making furious hand signals to him to shut up.

Sighing Sean turned back to the corporal. "Infecting someone without a lion's permission is pretty much a death sentence."

"I didn't need no lion's permission!"

"Actually, you did, and you got it, too. We just delegated it out. Now," Sean said, giving him a serious look. "Do you have any idea who and what I am?" he asked with a hint of a growl.

"I'm a tiger now! And I ain't afraid of no lion!"

"Oh, *shit*," Frank swore as Sean's hand lashed out while he shifted into his hybrid form. Leaning forward, he grabbed the corporal by the neck, then stood up quickly, dragging Lee towards him until they were nose to nose.

"I wouldn't do that if I were you," someone said as the other Marines stood up.

"Why not?"

"Because you'll only make him mad. Seriously, are you all stupid or something?"

Sean looked around at the others as the corporal grabbed his arm with both of his hands and tried to pry off his grip.

"Marines, *Sit*!" Sean growled at the others, putting a little of his lion essence into it.

They all sat, their faces showing their shock and surprise.

Sean turned back to look at the corporal. "What am I going to do with you?" he growled.

"Shut up!" Sean ordered as the corporal started to open his mouth. "That was a rhetorical question; you can look it up later if you don't know what it means." Sean pondered a moment. Obviously there were a lot of new lycans who hadn't had time to learn the lore and history of the lycan races. Also, with so many of them being made lately, they probably weren't getting half the attention they needed.

"Sir, can we…" Wyatt started to say.

"Quiet, I'm thinking," Sean growled.

The corporal's attempts to free himself were now getting a little more frantic.

"Sorry," Sean said and loosened his grip a little, letting the man breathe again, just as a bunch of Marines wearing officer insignia ran into the room.

Sean held up his free hand to them and then pointed to a few unoccupied chairs. Apparently *they* knew what a lion was, and they all parked their butts accordingly, while the marines sitting around the table started to look worried.

Betty gave a soft sob then.

Sighing, Sean turned to her. "I'm not going to hurt anybody, Betty. Especially not your friends.

But examples *do* have to be made, or next time I'll have to *kill* somebody," Sean said growling out the last. "Also, it's apparent that some of their training has been neglected, so I guess I need to deal with that now."

Looking back at Corporal Lee, Sean smiled. "You are going to get a sign. You are going to write on it: 'I've been a bad kitty'. You are going to put it around your neck, and you are going to shift into your tiger form and spent the next twenty-four hours visiting *all* the Marine barracks and units, where you will tell everybody exactly what happened, and that it is not wise to piss off a god.

"Oh, and yes, lions are your gods now. Understand?"

The corporal glared at him.

"I asked if you understood me, Corporal!" Sean growled and, again, put a little force into it.

The corporal's eyes got wide and he nodded.

"Wonderful. That's an *order*, and you can't shift back to human form until it's complete." Sean opened his hand, dropping Corporal Lee to the floor.

"Now, *go*!"

Lee went.

"Okay, for the rest of you," Sean said looking around the table. "You will finish your breakfast, then you will collect your weapons—unloaded of course—then you will shift into your animal forms and spend the next twelve hours field stripping and reassembling each of your firearms again and again, until you have it right."

"But that's impossible!"

"Well, after the first six hours you can do it in hybrid form, assuming you can achieve it by then.

"Oh, and you're going to do this once a day, every day, from now until you can achieve your hybrid form, understood?" Sean growled it out again and put some essence into the words, so they'd have no choice but to do what he told them.

"Yes, Sir!" they all chorused.

Sean smiled and looked at the officers. "There will be no further punishments assessed. Though you're free to yell at them later all you want. Now if you gentlemen," Sean motioned to the officers, "would follow me, I'd like to discuss some training issues."

Turning, Sean walked out of the room, heading for his workshop. Somewhere around here he had a new office, but damned if he could remember where the hell it was.

"Damn that Lee and his big mouth," one of the Marines muttered as the officers hurriedly followed Sean out of the mess.

"Yeah, we're screwed now," Wyatt said with a sigh. "I bet he assigns us every shit job he can find!"

Frank snorted. "He's already moved on. Sean isn't one for holding grudges. But you all did put your foot in it. Just be glad he wasn't in a bad mood."

"Bad mood? I gotta field strip a rifle with paws!"

Frank nodded. "Quickest way to integrate your two halves into one is to perform mundane tasks in your animal form. That's not punishment, that's *training*."

Wyatt blinked. "Oh!" Turning, he looked at the others. "Well, suck it up Marines, and finish your food, I guess we got training to do!"

Walking into his workshop, Sean noted that the four new machines had been moved out already. Going over to his workbench, he sat down and looked at the four officers who had followed him in.

"Okay, you need to get your folks some training here. If those guys are any indication, you're all a bit behind on learning how to shift into your hybrid form. We can't get you armored up with the good stuff until you can achieve that, okay?"

Sean looked at them as they all blinked.

"I thought you were going to chew us out for their behavior."

Sean identified him as Captain Yokota from his rank insignia and nametag.

"Yeah, well, I don't have time for that, and to be honest, what I did in there was probably a lot worse than beating him to within an inch of his life," Sean said with a smile, "but you guys need training, and it looks like you need to learn *what* you are now. Apparently a few things haven't sunk in, so you need to see to it that everyone is trained and in the know. Tell your commanding officer that this is an order from *me.* How you all want to deal with it is your business, as long as you start dealing with it *now.*"

"What do you want us to do?"

"Find an experienced lycan volunteer or two; ask Gloria Channing for help with that. That person, or persons, is then going to teach *all* of you about lycan history and customs. Make sure your people learn it. You're living in a fantasy world now, and the rules aren't what you grew up with.

"Now as for learning about shifting into your hybrid forms, you need to spend more time in your animal forms and listen to your animal more. Give it more control; you'll discover that it's really just you. Do things like what I ordered those guys to do, and you'll figure it out a lot faster than you have been.

"And most importantly of all…"

"Don't piss off any lions?" Captain Yokota suggested helpfully.

"Well, that too," Sean said with a grin, "but don't be afraid to ask the older hands and those born as lycans for help. I realize the alphas doing the infecting are all overwhelmed right now, and I feel guilty that I didn't realize it sooner. For the most part, folks will help you out."

"Are you really god?" Lieutenant Dougan asked.

Sean smiled. "Lions are the gods of the lycans. We created them, all of them. You're our children. That's why we have power over you. So while that makes me *a* god, we are not *the* god."

"Have you met him?"

"Who, God?" Sean asked.

Lieutenant Dougan nodded, a look of expectation on his face.

Sean shook his head. "No." He thought a moment, then added, "But I think my dad has."

Sean looked around the room. "If there are no other questions, you're dismissed. I've got work to do."

#

Chief Inspector Karl Weber looked around the farmhouse. Everyone there was looking back at him. What he was doing would most likely cost him his job, his pension, and perhaps even his freedom. But what was a man to do? He'd known these people most of his life and had served here for over two decades. They were his friends, his duty.

"So, what you're saying," said Peter's father, Reg, "is the very things that are attacking the Americans are now attacking us here as well? And we should leave?"

Karl nodded. "Yes, you should all go home; pack up and leave. Now. Not in the morning, not tomorrow afternoon. Now. This instant. Get your families and go."

"But, *why*?"

"Because we have no defense against these monsters, whatever they are. Normal weapons will not stop them."

Adele, from a farm down the road, spoke up, "But what about the government? Shouldn't we be asking them for help?"

"If the government knew I was here, I would be arrested and thrown in jail," Karl told them.

"What? How can that be?"

Several other people in the room protested as well.

"Because I have already been told that will happen to me, that is how it can be," Karl said and shook his head. "Someone obviously knows what's going on. I only discovered this because I caught Peter looking at the reports on the internet from America."

"I haven't seen any reports," Reg said.

"Neither have I," Karl agreed, nodding, "but Mr. Hoffner had special access set up through the technical company he worked for. The rest of us have all been very dependent on the same service, which I suspect makes it easy for us to be blocked."

"How are the Americans dealing with them?" Johan Riedel asked.

"They have a large lycan population, who are apparently able to stand up against these monsters and fight them," Karl said with a frown.

"So that law banning lycans from our country was not some strange moment of insanity from our government? Lycans are real?"

"Actually, I think that law was a very large act of insanity, now that I see what we're up against," Karl told them. "But yes, the lycans do exist. The Americans have gone so far as to recognize their existence, and I'm sure you have all seen the news about the attack on our embassy in the States by a group of them."

"And all this time I thought it was just a bunch of people in funny costumes," someone muttered in the back.

"So why isn't anyone doing anything about this?" Adele asked as Reg suddenly stood up.

"What are you doing?" she asked, turning towards him.

"Leaving. I suggest you all do the same. Chief Weber has told us if we stay, we will die, and no one can help us. I see no reason to doubt him."

"But my life is here! All of our lives are here!"

"No," Reg said slowly shaking his head, "our lives are now elsewhere. Only our deaths are here, like Marty and Gwen's."

"But monsters?" Johan said. "Do you really believe that?"

"I know over a dozen people have been brutally murdered and no one seems to be doing anything about it. That's good enough for me. I'll not risk my family, my wife, my children. It doesn't matter what it is, it's no longer safe here, and I will not return until it is!" Reg told them all as he walked over to the door.

Stopping a moment, he looked back at them, shook his head, and then left.

"Is there anything else you can tell us, Chief Inspector?" Adele asked.

"I've already said too much."

"Will you be leaving, too?" one of the others asked.

Karl shook his head. "It would look too suspicious if I were to go. Besides, my duty is here, to all of you. Now I must go warn others."

They watched as Karl put on his hat and left.

"What do you think?" Johan asked no one in particular. "Should we stay? Or should we go?"

"If we go, there will be trouble." Adele sighed.

"I think there will be trouble no matter what we do," said Sharon Mills, an old woman who had lived here since the forties, "but I've known Karl since he was a child. If he is willing to risk his career to warn us," she said sitting up as she looked around the room at everyone else, "we would be fools, ungrateful fools, to ignore it."

"Then I guess we're going," Adele said, getting up to leave.

The others nodded and, getting up, followed her out the door as they headed back to their own homes.

Shared Delusions

Pastor Cross looked around the room at a much smaller crowd than he'd come here with. None of the women where here, unfortunately. He'd heard the ones he'd shot had survived, but apparently those heathen lycans had had their way with them or something, as none of them had come back. Rumor had it even Geoffrey's hot little daughter was up there, living with them like a common whore.

Poor Geoffrey, Pastor Cross could only imagine what the man must be going through to have discovered not only that his daughter had sold him out, but that she was lying with those animals each night. That probably explained why he was the first to come back, and had rounded up as many of the others as he had.

"I'm glad to see all of you made it out on bail," Pastor Cross began. "Once again, we have our friends at the Anti-Lycan Society to thank for that. When they heard about our troubles, they were kind enough to send out a couple of their lawyers to get your bail reduced to something a bit more affordable."

"But we can't leave town," complained Cheranko, one of the newer members of the congregation.

"Why would you want to leave town?" Geoffrey said, his voice rough with the anger that always seemed to be consuming him these days. "The lycan scum are *here*!"

"So's your daughter…"

"I don't have a daughter!" Geoffrey yelled, jumping to his feet and threatening Cheranko with a fist. "She died out there with the rest of them. That's not my daughter! My daughter is *dead*!"

Cheranko nodded slowly, his face pale at the violence of Geoffrey's outburst.

Pastor Cross noticed several men frowning and nodding. He figured these were the men who'd had their sights set on Geoffrey's girl, and were equally upset that she'd been taken away from them.

He might be able to use that when the time came. He'd have to think about it. He'd also have to see about tracking down the men who hadn't come to tonight's meeting. While the women hadn't been charged by the local DA, their husbands had been, so they were stuck here, too, and even though the girls may have been corrupted, his bed was still rather cold and empty these nights.

Who knows? A little personal attention just might bring them back into the fold. No one was truly beyond redemption.

"Gentlemen," Pastor Cross said, raising his hands and motioning to them to settle down, bringing their eyes back to him. "Many of us lost somebody that day. None of us had any idea that the heathen unbelievers had grown so strong. That the devil had joined forces with them to give them such powers! But never fear, for we *shall* be victorious in the end, and the kingdom of heaven shall await ye all, because you are truly men of God, going about God's good work!"

He continued on for a few more minutes in a similar vein, until he had them all focused once more on him, and on doing the Lord's work.

"But how can we beat them?" asked George, one of his more trusted men, when he'd finished. "There are less of us now, and we don't even have any weapons anymore!"

"Did not the Good Lord provide for us before?" Pastor Cross asked.

George nodded slowly. "Yes, but…"

"But nothing!" Pastor Cross said loudly, but with a smile, to make sure everyone knew he wasn't casting doubts on George. He needed George, after all.

"Yes, I know times look hard for us all right now, but have faith in the Lord! He will provide! I have no doubts, and neither should you! When the time is right, he will reveal his plan to us, as was foretold! He will make his plans and his methods clear to you, through me, so that we may prevail against his heathen enemies! Have no doubts, and put your trust in the Lord!"

Pastor Cross smiled as they all nodded, looking hopeful once more, the beaten and lost expressions now gone from their faces.

"The ALS people have been kind enough to help with our getting this small hotel for the next few weeks," he continued. "Now, all of you, Mick has your room assignments. Geoffrey will keep you apprised of our meetings. But for now, go and rest. I know this has been a very trying time for you all."

Nodding, they all stood and went over to talk with Mick. Pastor Cross, meanwhile, left the room, heading into one of the back hallways.

"I heard what you told them," said Robert King, the Anti-Lycan Society man who had come, along with the lawyers, to help them out. "You really think you have a chance?"

"God will show us the way," Pastor Cross replied. "After all, he sent you here to help, did he not?"

Robert snorted. "We're here because *you* called us and offered to help repay those bastards for our dead members. God had nothing to do with it."

"The Lord works in mysterious ways," Pastor Cross replied with a smile.

"Oh, really? Tell me, was it the Lord who provided you with those women?" Robert said with a frown. He didn't like con men. He liked con men who believed the snake oil they were selling even less. "Cause if he did, I'm sure they'll all forgive you for what you did, right?"

Pastor Cross frowned. "I am the Lord's chosen, it is only right for me to spread my seed to whatever willing vessels the Lord sends my way. Now, are you here to insult me? Or do you wish to discuss business?"

Robert nodded slowly and held his tongue. He'd been sent out here with a mission, after all, and if these idiots were willing to follow a man who'd shot a bunch of their wives in the back after he'd knocked them up, they'd probably be willing to do this job, as well.

"Sorry," Robert said. "That was out of line."

"Better," Pastor Cross said with a smile. "Now, what weapons can you get us, and how soon?"

"That's the problem," Robert said, giving him a serious look. "No matter what kind of weapons I give you, they're not going to be stopped. We're dealing with trained soldiers, and they're a lot better with rifles than your people will ever be."

"Then what do you suggest?" Pastor Cross frowned. "Strong language?"

"Actually, we had an idea, but well, it will require great sacrifices by some of your faithful." Robert paused a moment, and then baited the hook.

"So great that I'm not sure if any of your people would be willing."

"My people will make any sacrifice I command them to!" Pastor Cross said, sounding indignant. "Do not doubt their faith, Mr. King! Now, what did you have in mind?"

Robert smiled to himself as another sucker took the bait and swallowed it whole.

"A bomb."

"A bomb? What's so dangerous about a bomb?"

"A big one, a truck bomb. Like those terrorists used in Oklahoma and New York. It'd mean the loss of one or two of your members if we want to be sure it's done right, but we could easily level their building in town."

"Or even take out enough of their compound in the hills if we made it big enough!" Pastor Cross said with a smile.

"I think the target in town would be a better one," Robert said with a dour look. "The compound is too open, success wouldn't be guaranteed. Their building in town, however, is much more vulnerable."

Pastor Cross smiled predatorily at him, reminding Robert quite suddenly of shark. "That's why you have *me*!" Cross chuckled nastily. "You think too small. Why do we have to pick a single target? Why not both?"

Robert blinked, leaning back a little in surprise at the sheer audacity of Cross's statement and his willingness to send his followers to their deaths. "Both?"

Cross nodded. "Both."

Robert pondered that a moment and then smiled. "Both is good."

#

Sean looked through his binoculars at the small gateway hovering a few inches over the sagebrush.

"Nothing's come through?" he asked Chad, who was standing next to him.

"Nope. Not a damn thing."

"Yet they fought us tooth and nail at the last big gate," Sean said, thinking about the one that had closed yesterday.

"Maybe they don't have the resources?" Max asked.

"Oh, they've got the resources," Estrella grumbled.

"I think they're not using them because their king doesn't know what to do with them," Chad said, speculating. "Think about it. Stell here told us the king never gets involved until the main gateway opens."

"So because he doesn't know how, he doesn't?" Max replied. "Sounds a bit too pat to me."

Chad shrugged. "We've been kicking his ass at the large gates where he can bring in all the power he wants. I've said it before; I think he's using them to get an idea of what he'll be up against when the main gateway opens. If that's the case, then he's not going to learn anything with these. He'll just be pissing away assets he could use when the next large one opens."

"Or maybe he's just trying to lull you into a false sense of security," Max countered. "So when he does strike through them, we're all caught off guard."

Chad smiled. "I admit the idea has merit. Besides which, it's good practice for the new troops, if nothing else."

"How many troops do we have now, anyway?" Sean asked.

"Quarter of a million, and growing fast."

"Any projections on how many we're going to end up with?"

"Between the reserves and the actives, I think we're going to have at least a half million here by July."

"Just how big is the US Army?" Max asked.

"Over a million," Chad told her, "with about another million in the reserves. Then of course there's the militia."

"Militia?"

"Every able-bodied male from like seventeen to forty-five."

"You're kidding me!"

"All of your men are in the military?" Estrella asked, also sounding surprised.

Sean nodded. "Yup, and for ninety percent of them, it's going to be a rude surprise if and when the government decides to call them up."

"It's an old law," Chad said, continuing. "Been on the books since the country was founded, and never taken off. Probably how they justify the draft, I don't know." Chad shrugged. "Law isn't exactly my thing. But when things start to go really crazy, I suspect we're going to see a very big increase in numbers."

"They've got millions on the other side," Estrella said in a soft voice. "Maybe ten million? More? I don't think we're going to be able to hold them off with just a million soldiers."

"We've got better weapons than they're used to," Chad pointed out.

"Perhaps, but they've got magic."

"We've got magic, too," Sean reminded her.

Estrella shook her head. "Not like they do. The demon kings and queens, their magic is different than ours. It comes from their followers, the ones bound to them. I've seen some of the things a demon lord can do, and a king has dozens, if not more, tied to him through each of the princes he controls."

"I guess we'll be finding out, then," Chad said. "It's not like they're going away."

"Don't forget that the race who built all the gate controllers beat them with technology," Sean pointed out.

"They still lost the second time around," Estrella countered.

"Because they didn't do a thorough job, nor did they keep their weapons around afterwards. We know better than to do that."

"Plus," Max said with a grin, "we *really* like our weapons!"

"So, what are our plans for the long term then?" Sean asked, turning to Chad.

"Fight the large gates, keep training and recruiting, and prepare for the main one. The logistics guys are telling me they're getting things converted over to iron, and there's a lot of interesting development going on to make sure we don't lose." Chad shrugged. "Other than that, until we're really into it, there's not much to say. They haven't shown us any new tricks since we blew their fort up."

Sean nodded. "How are things going with the magic users? You getting enough support?"

"I was a bit worried at first, but they seem to be warming up to the job. I just wish we had more of them. They've all been pretty unhappy about the lack of attacks coming from the small gates."

"What? Coming out here isn't worth their time?"

Max and Chad both laughed. "No, they're complaining because they're afraid they're not getting enough practice. I think Jack is working on setting up some sort of war games for them, using his lycans as the opposing forces."

"I'd been hoping we could steal a bunch of magic users from Europe to help us," Sean said, shaking his head, "but with the rumors coming out of Germany, I'm not so sure that's wise."

"Still no word on what's really going on there?"

Sean shook his head. "There aren't a lot of magic users in Eastern Europe; they all fled back when communism was running things. Most of the ones in Western Europe picked the really big cities, or the nicer climates to the south."

"What about the magical gangs?" Max asked.

"I've been told that someone is looking into it, but nothing beyond that."

"Well," Chad said, motioning for them to head down the other side of the rise away from the gate, "let's call in our ride and head back to base."

"Not worried about someone coming through?" Estrella asked.

"Not really. My people know what needs to be done, and it's only a small gate; I'm sure my captains can handle it. I got better things to do than just stare at a hole."

Sean had to agree; he'd come along today because he hadn't been out since the last large gate over a week ago. Estrella had been spending a lot of hours every day with Chad and Max going over everything she'd ever seen or learned about the enemy. Even Joseph Harrison from the Council of Eruditio had been coming up to the compound a couple times a week to ask her about the demons and life on the other side of the gateway. The only thing they hadn't been telling anybody about was Mahkiyoc Aan Drues, the being they'd met there who was the last of his race. The First had ordered them not to discuss that topic with anyone on Earth, only in the lion realm, where none of them could be overheard or spied upon.

"So what are your plans for the afternoon?" Estrella asked him as they got into the helicopter.

"I guess I need to meet with Deidre to go over finances," Sean grumbled.

"Right, finances." She chuckled.

"When she called me earlier, the message made it clear I had actual *work* to do."

"Oh, my poor boy. Reduced to doing actual work!" Estrella teased.

"I know, right? I'm a lion! Rawr!" Sean said with a grin. "I'm supposed to lie around all day, sleep, and get waited on hand and foot."

"Does that ever work for any of them?" Max interrupted.

"Once, I think. They all still tell each other stories about it!" Estrella giggled.

"Let me guess, Dad?" Sean asked.

Estrella laughed again. "Hardly. I think he's a, what's that word I heard last week? 'Workaholic?' I think mother would be delighted if he was to just lie down and ask to be waited on for a century or two."

"Why's that?" Max asked.

"Because if he's working, we're all supposed to be working, too."

"Now I know why you went through the gateway!" Sean laughed. "To get away from dad and get some time off!"

Estrella hauled off and punched Sean in the arm hard enough that if he hadn't been strapped into his seat, he probably would have fallen out of the helicopter.

"Not funny!" she growled.

"But is it true?" Sean teased back.

Estrella shook her head and grumbled, "That's why it's not funny."

"Okay, I'm sorry," Sean said and put an arm around her, pulled her close, and gave her a kiss. "I'll be sure to make it up to you tonight."

"Better," she said and leaned into him a bit. "You know, these helicopter things aren't so bad once you get used to them."

"I heard a rumor that Daelyn is learning to fly them?" Chad asked.

"Yeah." Sean nodded. "I think she finally found something more insane than that car of hers. Still, it's a good idea, I just wonder what she'll end up buying."

"You don't think she'll take one of the Black Hawks?"

"Not if there's something faster she can get her hands on. You gotta remember, her 'Cuda is *fast*. That thing is more like a low flying missile than a car."

They talked a bit more, but the flight back to the compound wasn't a long one, and a few minutes later Sean was walking into Deidre's office, which again reminded him that he had to see about finding where his own office was, now that he was no longer sharing with her. Apparently he was expected to do *work* when he was in his office now, instead of doing Deidre, he thought with a grin.

"Ah! Master Sean! You're here! Let's go."

"Go? Go where?"

"You need to inspect the building we bought."

"We bought a building?"

"The casino project? Remember? With your friend Steve and the head of the eastern pack, Claudia?"

Sean blinked, he'd forgotten all about that.

"Come," Deidre said, taking his hand and leading him out of the room. "Cali and Daelyn are waiting out by the car."

"We actually bought a building?"

"Actually, Claudia has had the building for ages, but the licensing is about to come through, so you need to be there as one of the principals."

"I thought I put my mother in charge of that?"

"You did. That's why we haven't bothered you until now," she told him as they got to the car. Deidre got in behind the driver's seat; Cali got in behind the passenger's. Getting in and closing the door, Sean leaned back into the seat as he felt Cali's fingers start to massage the back of his neck and lower scalp.

"You know, I have no idea where we're going?" Sean said as Daelyn pulled out of the parking lot and started flying down the driveway.

"Don't feel bad," Daelyn laughed, "I'd forgotten about it too!"

"Makes me wonder what else I've forgotten about," Sean said, looking out the window as the traffic flew by. "Hey, is it my imagination, or are there fewer cars on the road today?"

"People are startin' to notice that there's definitely somethin' going on out in the desert." Daelyn said while negotiating her way around a couple of slower vehicles. "So they're movin' out."

"Huh, took 'em long enough."

"Yeah, well, they got something now to drive it home that life's about ta' change on 'em."

"Oh? What?"

"Lemme show ya'."

Daelyn hit the exit ramp, slid the car around in a nice drift, and pulled off onto East 2nd.

"What am I looking for?" Sean asked as she slowed down and drove towards downtown. He was a little surprised that she hadn't grabbed the previous exit for 80 and just taken it down to Virginia.

"You'll see," was all she would say.

Nodding, Sean looked out the window. He tried to recall the last time he'd been downtown. It had been what? A few weeks ago, but that had been at night when they went out to dinner.

Daelyn pulled around a couple of Humvees, and then passed a few other transports he wasn't exactly familiar with. There were a lot of armed people on the streets now, a lot of them were in uniform, and a fair deal of the ones who weren't were in the new 'militia' outfit the governor had asked Sean's people to wear so the police would leave them alone.

But other than that, it seemed to be perfectly…

Sean stopped and turned to look out Daelyn's window, looking past her. There were quite a few armed people on that side of the street, as well. Then there were the military vehicles on the road they'd been passing going the other way.

"When the hell did the Army get here?" Sean asked, looking around some more.

Daelyn, Cali, and Deidre laughed. "When you brought them here?"

"But I thought we only had a quarter million…" Sean stopped and facepalmed. A quarter of a million people in a city of a quarter million was going to stand out, even if only a quarter of them were living in the city.

"It's more like a half million, my husband," Cali said from behind him. "There are still a lot of human soldiers who either have not been infected, do not wish to be infected..."

"Or failed the selection process to be infected," Deidre finished for her.

"It's startin' to look like there's a war on, ain't it?" Daelyn chuckled.

Sean nodded and continued to look around. "I guess you're right."

It only took another couple of minutes to get downtown, then they pulled into the back parking lot for an old office supply store. Or what Sean remembered as an old store. The place had once been a casino many years ago, and from the new signs on the front, it was about to become one once again.

"This must be the place Claudia bought?"

"From what I've been told, she's been sitting on it for several years now," Deidre said, "which is why the gaming commission was able to move so fast. You're required to have owned the property for at least two years prior to your application."

Getting out of the car, Sean helped Cali out of the back, then put one arm around Cali and the other around Daelyn. They headed into the building, with Deidre following close behind him. He wasn't surprised to see armed security at the door. He didn't recognize either of the men, who were both werewolves, but they recognized him immediately, and giving nods of their heads, one opened the door for him and showed him inside.

"Wow, they've been doing a lot of work in here," said Daelyn, who was used to working at casinos, looking around.

Sean had to agree. The place was freshly painted, and the many gaming tables appeared to be, if not new, then clean and in good repair. There was a small stage at the south end of the gaming room, with a couple of small platforms for lounge bands scattered throughout the room.

"The main stage is through that arch," Deidre said, pointing to one of the many exits from the gaming room.

"Been here before?" Sean asked her.

Deidre shook her head. "No, but I went over the plans several times with your mother."

"Hey! They got mechanical machines in here!" Daelyn said, pointing to the rows of slots.

"Yes, your uncle was quite helpful. Seems he had a lot in storage and was willing to rent them to us."

"I just felt a large drain on my bank account," Sean said, putting a hand to his heart.

"Thppt! I've probably worked on half of 'em. Maybe when this war thing is over, I can get me old job back!"

"You want to work on slot machines?" Cali asked.

Daelyn shrugged, but she was grinning. "It's a fun hobby. I like mechanical devices, and slot machines have all sorts of fascinating idiosyncrasies. The new ones are all just electronic garbage. Inside, they're all exactly the same."

"Come, the office is back this way," Deidre told them, and Sean followed, watching that nice butt of hers. He'd been in lots of casinos over the years, and with all the stuff on his plate, being part owner in one just wasn't all that exciting right now.

"Sean! Cali! Daelyn! Deidre!" Louise said as they entered the office of the general manager.

"Hi, Mom," Sean said, and hugged his mother after the girls each took a turn saying hello. She was dressed sharply in a very conservative suit, with a skirt instead of pants. "Looks like you really do know how to run a casino!"

Louise snorted. "I haven't started running it yet. Claudia and Steve's father are in the conference room with the lawyers and the regulators, getting everything ready to sign."

"What's Steve's dad doing here?"

"Steve gave him power of attorney to sign for him, seeing as he's stuck in DC."

"Ah," Sean stopped a moment and looked his mother over; she looked a lot younger these days. A *lot* younger.

"Sean?"

"Am I going crazy? Or are you getting younger?"

Louise smiled. "I told everyone I got a facelift, that *that* was the reason I was gone."

"I'm not following you, Mom."

"I'm half faerie, Sean. Faeries live a very long time. Being half one means I age a lot slower, and will live longer as well. The problem is, if I didn't appear to age, people would have gotten suspicious. So I used an illusion spell to make it look like I was aging."

"So you stopped using it?"

Louise nodded.

"Why didn't you stop using it earlier?"

"Because I only cast it about once a year. When it wore off a month ago, I decided not to bother casting it again."

Sean shook his head and wondered how he'd missed that? Then again, it wasn't like he looked at his mother that way. It was only seeing her dressed up like this that had caused it to stand out to him.

"So when is the casino going to open?"

"May 1st."

"Wow, that's less than a week away! Well, let's go sign, and then I guess it's back to work for all of us."

#

"So why are we driving to Utah?" Geoffrey asked, looking over at Pastor Cross; he'd been out of jail on bail for over a week now and was aching for something, *anything*, to do. George was currently driving; they'd been on the road for a couple of hours.

"To pick up a couple of trucks."

"What do we need them for?"

Pastor Cross smiled. "The good Lord has answered our prayers once again. He's going to provide us with a weapon those sinful heathen animals cannot stand against!"

Geoffrey blinked, surprised. "I thought it would be weeks before you'd figure something out?"

Pastor Cross laughed. "I told you he would provide, and though his methods may be confusing at times to us mere mortals who follow him, his plans were made clear to me several days ago. It just took convincing our erstwhile allies over at the ALS to gain their help. As they have also lost people to the heathen animal blasphemers, once they saw my plan, the good Lord must have moved their souls, because they immediately moved to help us."

"Praise God," George muttered.

Geoffrey nodded. "Yes, praise the Lord. So what is your plan, Pastor?"

"We're going to make two truck bombs using fertilizer and diesel fuel."

"ANFO?" George asked from behind the wheel. "I've heard that's pretty powerful stuff!"

Pastor Cross nodded and smiled. "Very cheap and hard to trace, too. Especially in farming towns like we have all over the west coast."

"So why didn't we just rent a couple of trucks?" Geoffrey asked.

Pastor Cross frowned. "That's been done several times now, and each time it led to the police catching those involved."

"Well, won't buying them have the same effect?"

"These have been purchased on the black market, for cash. If they manage to trace them anywhere, it's the ALS that'll have to worry, not us."

"Will they have the stuff mixed up for us?" George asked. "Not sure if I want to be driving a huge bomb back over this highway."

Pastor Cross shook his head. "Both will be empty. We're going to need to build a large bin in the back of one truck to hold the mixture first."

"What about the second one?"

"The second one is a tanker truck," Pastor Cross said and smiled slowly. "We're going to need something especially large if we're going to destroy their ranch up in the hills and kill their false god."

Geoffrey laughed. "Can I drive it? Oh, to see the look on their faces when I bust down those gates!"

George took a quick look over at Geoffrey. "Dude, you crazy? You drive that in there, and you won't be coming out."

"They took my daughter, George. They took all I had, I've got nothing left. Besides, I do this and I'll be sitting at the Lord's own table come dinnertime! Maybe it'll make up for some of the things I did back before I heard the Word of God."

Pastor Cross could have cheered. He'd been hoping someone would step up to drive the trucks without him having to exert his considerable influence. That Geoffrey would immediately ask to be one of his martyrs was definitely a sign from God. Geoffrey was respected by everyone; that he'd put his life on the line for this would not be missed by the rest of the congregation.

Placing a sober expression on his face to hide the inner joy he was feeling, Pastor Cross turned to Geoffrey.

"Are you sure you want to do this? This is dangerous job, Geoffrey, and George is right. It will be a one-way journey."

"A one-way journey that kills the blasphemers, achieves the Lord's goals, and will send me to heaven, right, Pastor?"

Pastor Cross nodded slowly. "Yes, Geoffrey, doing this will definitely put you in the Lord's favor. As the first among my flock, if you wish to perform this duty, I will not gainsay your decision, for all that you will be missed. A man must follow his destiny, and any destiny that brings one closer to the Lord is one that I will praise."

Geoffrey smiled and leaned back in his seat. It felt like a great weight had been taken from his shoulders. What had happened with Betty, that had bothered him. The rumors he was hearing had bothered him even more. This simple act would expunge his mistakes. It would mean his end, but he didn't see that he had much of a future in this world anymore.

And he would be doing God's work.

"Thanks, Pastor Cross," Geoffrey said. "Thank you very much."

George shook his head. "You're a better man than me, Geoffrey. I don't think I could do that."

"With me gone, the pastor here is going to need somebody to step up; it's better that you don't go," Geoffrey agreed.

"But then who will drive the other truck?"

"Cheranko."

"Him?" George asked, surprised. Even Pastor Cross's eyebrows went up at the suggestion.

"He's a good man; he's just young. He's here because he wanted to do something important with his life. I don't think he'll be all that hard to convince."

"Thank you for that insight," Pastor Cross said. "I hadn't considered him because of how new he is to the congregation. But if you think he'd be interested, then I'll certainly talk to him once we're back in Reno."

Unconscious Alliance

"Yes, Madam Investigator, you wished to see me?" Karl asked as he walked into the temporary office Hannah was using.

"Yes, Chief Inspector. A most curious thing has happened."

Karl gave her a surprised look. "We've had a breakthrough in the case?"

Hannah frowned at him. "As much as I wish that were so, that's not what has happened. I've been informed by several of my people that they're seeing a large exodus of people from this area."

"Excuse me, Madam Investigator? An *exodus*?"

"Exactly that, Chief Inspector. So I got in my car and spent the morning driving around the farms and other houses in the country. Do you know what I found?"

Karl shook his head.

"Everyone had packed up and left. When I went into town, I noticed quite a few of the homes were empty, and several people were packing up and leaving."

"That is unusual, Madam," Karl agreed.

"Do you know what they said when I asked them why they were leaving?"

"No, Madam, I do not."

"They said that our lack of progress on those recent murders had led them to decide to go on holiday. That they would be back once the ones responsible had been apprehended."

Karl nodded and kept his face straight. She had nothing, and he wasn't going to give her anything now.

"Most curious, Madam."

"And what would your thoughts on the matter be?"

"That if our superiors back in Berlin were to find out just how badly we've lost the faith of the locals, our jobs would be in jeopardy."

Karl was surprised then as Hannah smiled at him.

"My thoughts *exactly*, Chief Inspector. My thoughts exactly. I'm glad we're seeing eye-to-eye on this at least. So let's not go mentioning this in any of our reports to our superiors, okay?"

"Of course, Madam Investigator."

"Please, call me Hannah, Karl. As much as this loss of faith concerns me, with fewer people in the area now, I'm sure this will make solving our case that much easier."

"One can only hope, Hannah," Karl said, shaking his head. "One can only hope. I think I'll take a run out there, look over the properties, and make a list of who's gone, so I can alert my staff to keep an eye on those homes."

"Worried about robberies?"

"Actually, I'm more worried that our killers might move into one of them."

"You think they might?"

"We know they're not staying in any of the hotels around here. Living in a house might appeal to them."

Hannah nodded slowly. "I hadn't thought about that. It would certainly make dealing with them easier if we knew where to look."

"I just hope your bosses will send us some support. I'm thinking our old riot vests, truncheons, and nine millimeters aren't going to be enough for this group."

"I'd have to agree with you there, Karl. I'll make some phone calls and see if I can't get some action from Berlin. I'll tell them we have a possible lead, but we're going to need help taking these people down."

Karl gave a relieved smile; it wasn't perfect, and it wasn't what he'd been expecting when he was called in here, but it was far and away better than anything he'd hoped for.

"Have a good day then, Hannah."

"You too, Karl."

Karl pulled up by the Becker place when he saw something moving through one of the windows. The Beckers had left all their shades open, and whoever was inside hadn't thought to close them.

"Sofia," he called over his radio to dispatch, "this is Karl. I'm at the Becker place. I need to investigate something."

"You want me to send someone out there to back you up?"

"Only if you haven't heard from me in a few minutes. For all I know, they forgot to let their cat out."

"Okay, but do let us know."

"Of course," Karl said. He opened the door and got out, making sure not to close it behind him. If there was someone inside, he didn't want to alert them. And if it was what he feared, he sure didn't want to have to waste any time opening the door to get away.

He thought about drawing his pistol, but he remembered that the police officer in America hadn't had any success with that. Instead, he grabbed his pepper spray. The police-issued version was quite vicious, and hopefully it would give him enough time to escape.

Looking around, he decided to approach the house from the east, using the trees for cover. That side of the house was in the shade, so with any luck, he could peek inside one of the windows without giving himself away.

Creeping forward slowly and being careful where he put his feet, he managed to get to the side of the house without making any noise or being discovered. Flattening himself against the side of the house, he looked around carefully to make sure he was still undiscovered, then he slowly moved towards one of the windows. Sticking his head around the corner, he glanced inside.

There was something there.

It took him a moment; he'd never seen anything like it, and his mind was taking a moment. It was large, it walked on two legs, and it was covered in fur from the top of its head down to its feet. It almost looked like a bear, but it was all the wrong shape, the arms looked like arms, not legs, and it was far too well balanced.

It turned towards him, and he quickly pulled back from the window and found himself staring right into the face of the biggest damn lion he'd ever seen, not that he'd seen more than the one that used to be at the zoo.

He didn't even hesitate; he brought up the pepper spray.

"Wait!"

Pushing the plunger on the spray bottle he let the lion have it full in the face!

The lion made a noise between a scream and a roar as Karl felt something grab his wrist and pull it down, moving the spray away from the lion's face.

"Otto!" the lion growled.

Karl tried to pull away from the lion, which he suddenly realized wasn't a lion. Well, not exactly. It was big, and it was covered in tawny fur, those parts of it that weren't concealed by a nice dress shirt with a pair of slacks… Looking around in a panic, he thought something here wasn't quite right. His right arm was immobilized so he couldn't reach his pistol easily, so he started flailing around with his left arm to see if he could get it to let go of him. It was growling and snarling and yanking him back and forth as it tried to deal with the face full of pepper spray.

Apparently pepper spray worked well on, well, whatever this thing was, though not good enough to make it turn him loose.

"Otto!" the lion growled again, louder.

Karl finally managed to get a grip on his pistol, though the retention hold was giving him problems.

"Karl!" a familiar voice shouted. "Don't shoot him; you'll just piss him off!"

Looking around, Karl saw Otto Hoffner standing there, nude.

"Otto?" he said, looking surprised.

"Yeah, it's me, Otto."

"Why aren't you wearing any clothing?"

"Because you wouldn't recognize me otherwise. You can let him go, Raban."

"Only if he stops with that damn pepper spray! Find me a hose or something!"

"What's going on here?" Karl asked, looking back and forth between the two of them. "Do you know him?"

"Yes, Karl. I know him. Now drop the pepper spray and let's find the hose. I'll answer all of your questions, after we deal with Raban."

Karl felt the hand holding him release him, and looking back at 'Raban', there was no longer a lion *thing* standing there. Instead it was a very Nordic looking, middle-aged man, with conservatively cut short brown hair. His eyes were closed, and mucus was pouring out of his nose as his eyes wept tears.

"What is going on?" Karl said, starting to wonder what he'd gotten himself into.

"Water first!" Raban growled. "Explanations second!"

"Come on," Otto said, grabbing Raban's arm, dragging him into the house, and into the kitchen, where he took the sprayer facet and started rinsing out Raban's eyes.

"Okay," Otto said as Raban grabbed the sprayer and started washing his own face. "You can ask questions while I go look for a towel."

"Why are you naked?" Karl asked.

"Because I don't have a collar yet, and shifting ruins my clothes still."

"Shifting?"

"I'm a werewolf, Karl. So's Marge and the kids."

"You left because of the law?"

"No, we left because the lions ordered us all out of Germany."

"Why'd…" Karl stopped that train of thought, it wasn't important. Well, not yet at least. "Why are you here?"

Otto found a towel in the bathroom and started back towards the kitchen. "We heard a rumor that there were demons here. While the lions don't want any lycans in Germany, Raban thought it might be a good idea for someone to investigate."

Karl sighed. "They're here, alright."

"What!" Raban's head came up, and while Karl could see his eyes were still red and weeping, he fixed his gaze on him. "Where are they? Have you seen them?"

"I've seen what they've left behind," Karl said with a heavy sigh. "We don't know where they are yet. I was able to convince most of the locals to get out before they were killed, too."

"What's the government saying?"

"They're covering it up. They sent out a young gung-ho political type who's far more worried about her career than she is anything else."

"Who died?" Otto asked.

"The Youngs were killed, all of them. Same for the Ulmens, and the Schmidts."

Otto dropped down into a chair, shaking his head.

"Do you think you could put some clothes on?"

Otto's body just… *transformed* would be the only way Karl could have described it, and suddenly there was a very large werewolf sitting in the chair instead.

"Better?"

Karl gulped. "A little. Though I will say you look better than the ones in those movies. Where are your clothes?"

"We snuck in on four legs. I left mine in my car back on the road near the Irvings'."

"I'll take your word for it," Karl said slowly.

Raban took the towel and started to dry himself off.

"Damn, you ruined my shirt!" he complained.

"I almost ruined my pants," Karl said, looking back at him. "What did you expect to happen?"

"Not that, obviously. Here, catch."

Karl caught the large coin Raban tossed him.

"What's this?"

"A magical charm. Keep it on you at all times. Better yet, wear it on a chain and *never take it off.*"

"Why?"

"Because humans are a quick and easy meal to a demon. You can't withstand them; they simply take over your mind and rip out your soul."

"And this will stop them?"

Raban shrugged. "No idea. We haven't experimented with it, as if it doesn't work the subject would die. But it will protect you from most mind spells, so it might give you a chance to run away."

Karl nodded and looked at the coin. It had a lion's head stamped on one side, with the name 'Valens' inscribed on the back over what looked like a city's skyline. There was also a small hole near one edge, so you could affix it to a chain.

Slipping it into his pocket, Karl looked up at Raban. "Thank you, though I hope I won't be needing it. But that does bring up another question: How do you kill these things?"

"Iron works."

"So does fire," Otto added. "But you'd be better off running away, as Raban said."

"Why?"

"They don't just kill you, Karl. They eat your *soul*. Your immortal soul."

"I always thought souls were a myth?"

"Right up there with werewolves, magic, and demons, right?" Otto said, causing Raban to laugh.

"Come, you can take us to the homes of the people who were killed so we can try and figure out what we're dealing with," Raban said.

"What if we run into the demons?"

"They can't affect Lycans. We'll deal with them while you run."

Otto suddenly transformed again, and there was a rather large wolf standing in the kitchen.

"This way if anyone sees him with us, they'll just mistake him for a dog," Raban said. "Now, let's go."

§

Sean opened his eyes and stretched, his forepaws out before him as he curled his toes and bent his back, before he shook his head, causing his mane to flare out as his mouth snapped closed and he looked around for the First.

"I really need to spend more time as a lion," Sean grumbled to himself as he spotted the First and padded over towards him.

"Did I hear you right?" the First said as Sean came up to him, and they head-butted lightly.

Sean grumbled and plopped down next to him. "Yeah, the last week has been all work and very little play. I had to bust my ass to get those machines done for you…"

"Thank you very much for that, by the way," the First said. "We've already put them into production."

"Then I had to deal with some upstart Marines who apparently haven't been getting educated. That led to a couple of days of going around to *all* the new recruits and finding out that no one had given any thought at all to teaching these people their new history."

"Someone stood up to you, did they?"

Sean snorted. "Someone damn near put their foot in it so far I'd have had to take their head off. I nipped that in the bud right fast. But still, it shouldn't have happened."

"Combat troops do tend to be cocky, Son. That's why they're combat troops."

"Yeah, I know, but let's be honest here, I can do the thousand-yard-stare with the best of them these days. I guess people see that I'm young, and they figure I'm also inexperienced."

"Maybe you should stick to your hybrid form? Or even your lion form?"

Sean rolled over on his back and stretched again while he considered that. "You're probably right," Sean said with a sigh, "but I get tired of having to duck every time I go through a doorway. I think I've hit the one coming out of the bedroom enough to have made a permanent dent in the shape of my forehead there."

The First laughed at that. "How're the wives?"

"They're well. I think Roxy misses you, just a little."

"Oh?"

"She liked matching wits with you."

"She did?" the First said, looking surprised.

"Well, yeah. Of course she did. She always won, didn't she?"

Now it was the First's turn to snort.

Sean smiled at him, then rolled back over. "So, what's going on in Germany?"

"We sent Raban in."

"Who's that?"

"One of mine and Keairra's. He's spent a lot of time in Europe, so he knows the lay of the land there pretty well. There're definitely demons in the southern part of Germany, but he doesn't think it's a large party. They've only taken out a couple of farms. A lot of the remaining people have fled."

"What's the government doing?"

"Hiding it."

"What!" Sean said, shocked.

"They're hiding it. Raban talked to one of the chief inspectors in the area, and he told them they sent a higher-ranking person to shut down any talk about it and pretty much cover it up."

"Well, that's not good. Do you think the German government has been taken over?"

"That's what I suspect," the First said with a shake of his head. "All the governments in Europe, and even Asia, have the same spells and wards on their buildings as you saw here on your White House and Congress. At least the ones the leaders live or work in. But Germany's got destroyed in the war, and when they were finally rebuilt," the First shook his head again, "they didn't put them in. I guess they felt they had moved beyond all those old superstitions and other 'crazy' beliefs."

Sean thought about that. "You know, that may be the real reason they focused on Germany. The gateway opening there may just be a happy coincidence for them."

The First conceded the point with a nod.

"So what are we going to do about Germany?"

"You mean what am *I* going to do about Germany," the First said with a laugh.

Sean laughed as well. "Yeah, I've been threatened with all sorts of violence and mayhem if I ever leave Reno again without a good reason. Have you seen the numbers on the lycans lately?"

"Yes, we're about two and a half million now."

"That's not all my people, is it?"

"No, when word got out that your president had approved of your recruiting, other governments started looking into it as well. It's not going as fast for them, because we have to vet everybody. We haven't put in that high-speed process you've got going. The only big surprise has been the Swiss."

"Why's that?"

"They're going into it in a big way. Apparently, the idea of werewolves is really big in certain parts of Switzerland."

"Really?"

"Yup. Thankfully we have more lions living there right now, because of all the ones who left Germany. So they're getting a lot of help."

"Didn't you once tell me the number of lions that can exist depends on how many lycans are alive?"

The First nodded. "We could easily double our numbers right now. But then of course, I'd start to feel lonely here by myself," he said with a grin.

"Maybe you should see about rejoining the world?"

"This thing will be over before I'd be old enough to be a part of it."

"You know I miss you, Dad. It'd be nice to have you around."

"Maybe after we win the war, I'll consider it."

"Speaking of the war, the last time they were serious about it, how bad did it get?"

"Not as bad as it's going to be this time. We had a few lords come through, and we managed to kill most of them. We didn't get any princes, queens, or kings that time. The thing was, there were a *lot* fewer people then, so we really didn't have to watch all the gates, just the ones closest to the main population centers."

"Weren't you worried about them setting up a permanent base?"

"They never tried to. There wasn't enough food for them."

Sean nodded. "You know, I think Chad's right. I think we're going to have to go *there* if we ever hope to put an end to this thing."

"We've been discussing it. He may be right."

"We?"

"My advisors."

"You have advisors?" Sean said, shocked.

"Who do you think those lions are who are always sitting around talking to me when you show up?"

Sean grinned at him. "Suck ups?"

The First scowled at him, then swatted him on the nose with a paw.

"Really now, Son." He sighed.

"What? You've always claimed you ruled with an iron fist. 'My way, or else!' and all that kind of thing."

"That's just to keep you young ones in line. Most of the older ones have had some decent ideas now and again. So we sit around and talk. Which reminds me. How is Chad's weapon research coming along?"

"Which one?"

"The one to find a working cartridge for the other side of the gateways."

"Oh! Black powder works over there."

"So just a change in ammunition?"

"Wellllll, according to our firearms experts, you're not going to get very far with any kind of modern automatic rifle using black powder. It's pretty filthy and will clog the gas ports. So we're thinking lever action rifles with big ass cartridges. That or bolt action. Something simple."

"I'll talk to Ceithir about it; she's well tied into to manufacturing in China."

"Ceithir?"

"My younger sister, the one you were making eyes at that time."

"Well, in my defense, she is cute."

The First laughed. "Don't be fooled by looks. She's almost as nasty and vicious as I am. Sometimes she even makes Keairra look reasonable. Besides, she's probably just a bit too old for you."

"I'll be sure to tell her you said that!" Sean said and laughed. "Anything else I need to know?"

"I think that's enough for tonight. Sleep well, Son."

"Night, Dad."

Rinse & Repeat

Sean stretched and looked around the room. "Okay, so we got another small gateway yesterday. Anybody got anything new to discuss?"

Gloria Channing, Roxy's mom and the newly appointed training head, spoke up, "I've got a training program running, and I'm projecting we'll have everyone grounded in the basics by this Sunday."

"That quick?"

Gloria gave a curt nod. "It's not like the basics are that big of a deal. Everyone who was born a lycan knows them, and even if you've been turned, once you've mastered them, it's not that hard to explain them to someone else."

"Still, I'd have thought the manpower issue would have slowed you down."

"Pfft! Not a problem. I'm the mother-in-law of the lion in charge. When I ask you to volunteer, you volunteer."

"That's not exactly what's meant by 'volunteering', you know," Max pointed out.

"Hey, if you don't move fast enough when I'm looking for help, that's volunteering in my book!"

"Mom," Roxy said with a sigh, "you're a cheetah; *nothing* moves fast enough."

Gloria gave a truly evil smile then, making Sean wonder who was the real power in the Channing household. "I know."

"Well, at least I know where Rox gets it from," Sean whispered to Daelyn, and then tried not to flinch as Roxy kicked him under the table and Daelyn snickered.

"Still," Sean said, speaking up, "that's good. How are we on the ALS front? I know Steve is still having issues with them in DC, but has anyone seen any of them around Reno at all?"

"Far as I can tell," Bill said, "they're staying well away from Reno. A lot of their people were killed in the attack here, and brave they are *not*. These aren't people who'll normally engage in any violence, unless there's almost no risk at all to themselves."

"What about the DC attack?" Daelyn asked.

"Sean and the others were on the way back from the Whitehouse. Weapons aren't allowed there, so they thought they'd have superiority. They didn't realize that there were magic users along, nor what they could do." Bill gave a small shrug. "I also suspect they either didn't know about the security teams that follow Sean, Steve, and the rest everywhere, or they were told they weren't there that day."

"As I understand it," Colonel Jack Kennedy said, "they're mostly rich, bored kids and college grads who can't find a job and think it's everyone else's fault. They just jump from cause to cause to cause."

"That's not really far from the truth," Bill agreed. "But they do have some smart and powerful people backing them who have money."

"Like Germany," Sean grumbled.

"Germany is just the latest in a long string of users and abusers, I'm sure." Bill sighed. "Some folks are just too easily fooled. Or enjoy using others too much for their own good."

"Sounds like magic users all over again!" Peg said with a grin.

"Well, they're Steve's problem right now, more than ours," Sean said. "So let's get back to the war. We've got," he looked over at the large schedule painted on the wall, "twenty-one more gateways until the main event. Statistically, five or six of them should be large gateways. I'll admit this is starting to get boring; we're fighting the same damn fight every few days, with no end in sight."

"Yeah, the waiting is kind of getting to me, and the troops, too," Chad admitted. "There's only so much planning and practicing you can do. I've started cutting people loose on twenty-four hour passes after each gate closes. Told my commanders to make sure people get time off."

"Well, the casinos in town will sure enjoy that!" Peg said.

"So will the whorehouses!" Jolene added with a laugh.

"I'm waiting for those four Stew brought back to open one." Sean sighed.

"Why? Are you looking to try them out?" Cali asked.

"If I wanted to, I already would have. I am seriously *not* interested in those girls. I mean, come on; seven is a lucky number, why would I ever want to go for eight?" Sean said, turning to smile at Cali.

"How have things been going with the city?" Jack asked, looking over at Bill.

"They haven't been going as well as I'd like. I've asked Sean to start coming to the meetings with me."

"Oh?"

Sean gave a nod. "I'm not looking forward to it, I've already got enough going on to keep me busy, but apparently they want 'the man in charge' or some such bull."

"But," Bill added, "the mayor has been doing what she can to help us. It's just some of the other city council members and department heads who seem to be balking."

"So hopefully I won't have to do more than show up a few times and everything will be fine," Sean said with a smile.

"Have we heard anything about Germany?" Claudia asked.

"Just that they've got djevels and the government is covering them up. But that's not our problem, just like South America isn't our problem. So let's not go on worrying about it."

"Don't our troops returning from the Middle East have to go through there though?"

"All the bases in Germany now have a high percentage of lycans," Jack said. "Same is true for our bases in England and other countries in that area."

"I've looked at the numbers," Sean said. "We're getting large numbers of lycans recruited every day now. We're closing in on three million."

"You know how many lycans there are?" Claudia asked, looking surprised.

"Yup, to the exact number. It's a lion thing," he added and winked.

"Well," Deidre said, getting everyone's attention, "if nothing else needs discussing, then I guess we need to go over financials."

Just them the alert went off.

"Saved by the bell!" Sean laughed as several of the monitors came to life, showing pictures of the latest gateway.

It was one of the big ones.

"Uh-oh," Chad said, getting up, "I need to get out there."

"Yeah, I think I better go with you," Sean said, getting up as well. "Adam, you're with me. Let's go armor up."

Sean left the room at a trot, with Adam on his heels. The conference room wasn't all that far from the armory, fortunately.

"I'm starting to feel like I've been doing this forever." Adam sighed as they ran inside to where their armor and weapons were stored. "Must be worse for you; it's been what, eight months now?"

"Damned if I can remember," Sean said, quickly stripping out of his clothes and pulling on his new set of fey armor. "Since sometime last August."

"I can just imagine what we're going to be thinking three years from now, when this is finally over."

Sean laughed. "I'm sure we'll either be bitching about missing the 'good old days', or we'll be complaining about only having a thousand years off until the next one!"

"Yeah, that sounds a lot like last time," Adam agreed. Finishing up with his armor, he grabbed his weapons harness and ammo belt. "Least we're a lot better armed and supplied than last time."

Sean nodded, grabbed his own stuff, and they ran out to the helicopter were the troops were loading. Once inside, they quickly took off and headed for the latest gateway.

"Any word on this gateway, Trey?" Sean asked their pilot.

"There's a lot of demons coming out of it already, and they're digging in. Chad can't use the artillery because we're all flying into the area, so he's ordered a few air strikes to try to keep them occupied as we get set up."

"So basically it's business as usual."

"Well, the air strikes are new!"

Adam grumbled, "Yeah, but so is their digging in. Guess this is going to be one where we'll all be expected to earn our keep."

"Wait! We're getting paid for this!" one of the wolves, Sean wasn't sure who, spoke up.

"Dude, did you think all that kibble we were shoving down your throat was *free*?" Adam snapped back. "Now behave yourself, or we're putting you back on the store brand! No more 'Taste of the Wild' for you, my friend."

"I don't know, I kinda prefer the Kirkland brand," someone else muttered.

Sean chuckled. "I'm afraid to ask how you even know what that tastes like."

"We all do stupid things when we're kids," Frank laughed, "but if you want bad, try that crap they sell in the grocery stores!"

Shaking his head, Sean listened to them with half an ear as they compared brand names. The rest of his attention was looking out the window as they came in low to their landing zone.

"Ten seconds!" Trey called out, and the doors slid open and everyone grabbed the releases on the buckles of their harnesses as Trey flared out over the ground, then they rolled out of the helicopter before it had even come to a full stop.

By the time Sean had landed on his feet, Trey was already out of sight.

"Let's get up to that ridgeline and see what we're dealing with," Sean said and ran up the side of the hill with the others following. Dropping to his hands and knees before his head cleared the top of the rise, he crawled the last few feet and peered over the top cautiously.

"Doesn't look too bad," Hunter said from his left.

"They're serious about digging in this time," Adam said.

"Which means they're not watching us that much," Hunter agreed, then turned and looked to either side. "Well, this is as good a place as any, right, Boss?"

Sean nodded. "Set 'em up."

"Okay, everyone! You know the drill! Dig in. I want two weapons emplacements dug out after you finish the basic trench. We may not need them, but I'd rather not be digging them under fire if someone decides to move some heavy gear in! Get to work!"

"You know, that's one of the great things about being a lion," Adam said in a low voice. "No digging."

"I can get you a shovel if you want one," Hunter teased.

"And I can order you to put on a skirt and sing a luau," Adam teased back.

"Not if I order you to do it first," Sean said with a snort. "Besides, if we called any of the boars around here a pig, they'd probably gut all three of us."

Hunter laughed. "Yeah, they sure are tough sons of bitches. They just *look* slow."

Sean got out his binoculars and started looking at what was going on down at the base of the gateway. They were digging in down there as fast as they could, alright.

"Hunter, have our snipers start picking off people down there," Sean said as he continued to watch. He was looking for anyone who appeared to be casting spells or doing anything else magical.

"What are you doing, Sean?" Chad's voice came over the radio.

"Looking for magic users. I don't see any down there yet, but I might be wrong."

"You think they're up to something?"

"They're *always* up to something, you know that."

"Good point. I'll order harassing fire from the others."

"When can we expect artillery?"

"Five minutes after the last helo clears the area. That's why I wanted folks to concentrate on digging in."

"How long are you going to shell them for?"

"An hour the first time around. Then we'll let up and see what happens next."

"Sounds good."

"You think they're up to something in particular, don't you?" Adam asked Sean as he finished talking to Chad.

Sean nodded. "Yeah, I do. But let's just wait and see what happens, I wouldn't want to jinx it."

"You mean you wouldn't want to be wrong!" Adam said with a snicker.

"Well, yeah, I'm a lion now. Can't go being wrong, can I? What would the First say?"

"That you're learning. Well, might as well break out a shovel and help the others."

"Really?" Sean said surprised.

"It's part of my charm," Adam said, grinning. "Besides, all the hard work's done already."

When the shelling started a half hour later, Sean took partial cover in one of the trenches, but continued watching through the binoculars.

"This is where it gets really interesting," he told Adam between explosions.

"Why's that?"

"Because I don't think they're going to be using any magic."

"Why," Adam paused as another shell landed, "wouldn't they?"

"Because what good would it do them?" Another shell struck, knocking down the simple earthen wall the demons had started to build. "Once the gate closes, without constant reinforcements, they just won't be able to hold it."

Another shell hit.

"So why even try?"

"That's a good question, isn't it? Why even try…"

"You're starting to sound like Chad, you know."

A shell landed right in one of the ditches then, blowing up a huge pile of dirt, and quite a few bodies.

Sean laughed. "Yeah, too much time listening to him go on about tactics. But I'm looking at this like one of the games we used to play." Another shell hit, this one just outside the border of the construction going on. "I think I'm starting to see a method to this madness, and I think they've moved on to gathering data."

"All I know is, I'm seeing lots of body parts down there."

Another shell, and almost immediately after, a group swarmed out of one of the trenches to start rebuilding the earthen wall. Another shell hit right in the middle of them, killing them all. A moment later, another group started in on the same job.

"I can't understand why they're still trying to build and not waiting for the shelling to stop!" Adam said with an exasperated sigh.

"They have unlimited manpower. I wouldn't stop, either. It's an experiment."

"An experiment?"

"They want to see what they can build, without magic, if they just keep throwing bodies at it."

"Why would they do that?"

Sean put down the binoculars and looked at Adam. "Because once the main gateway opens, they'll have unlimited reinforcements and resupply. If they just keep throwing bodies at the problem, bodies they'll never run out of, sooner or later they'll get their fort built."

"But why aren't they using magic, then?"

"Oh, I'm sure that they will, eventually. But I don't think they're going to be doing it this time."

"Think Chad knows?"

"Let's find out," Sean said. Calling Chad on the radio, he shared his thoughts with him.

"I think you're right," Chad agreed. "I was starting to come to the same conclusion, because it's the only thing that really makes sense. Now the question is: What do we do about it?"

"How about never shelling them for more than thirty minutes at a time?" Sean suggested.

"Better yet," Adam added, "how about not shelling them at night? Make them think if we can't see them, we can't hit them."

Chad laughed over the radio. "You know what? Both of those are good. But that means they're going to get a lot of building done once the sun goes down."

"Bring up some heavy machine guns, a couple of howitzers, and give everyone lots and lots of hand grenades," Sean suggested. "We can keep their lives interesting during the night, and when the morning comes, we hit them with a really heavy barrage."

"Think they'll know we're messing with them?" Adam asked.

"No idea," Chad replied, "but how many people really know what the military is capable of these days? They've been possessing and dealing primarily with politicians. Otherwise they wouldn't be doing these little experiments."

"I'm wondering if we're still going to have to worry about a breakout once their fort is done," Sean said.

"I'm planning on it," Chad confessed. "But we have all day to get ready for it. So let's get everyone set up to deal with it before the sun sets."

The first night nothing happened, beyond them finishing all the berms and starting on the building. The machineguns and the cannons, along with a number of raids, kept the fort from making much progress, and come the morning the artillery knocked a lot of it back down.

But not all.

By the time the sun was starting to set at the end of the second day, Sean noticed they'd actually made a small amount of progress on their fort, and were fixing the damaged berms fairly quickly now.

"I think they're going to go for it tonight," he radioed Chad.

"I agree. What's your reasoning?"

"This is just too good an opportunity for them to get some djevels past our defenses and out into the area in general."

"You know, if I start shelling them after the sun sets, it just ruins all the work we've done here so far."

"I know," Sean agreed, "so I think we need to warn everyone that we're going to have a pretty nasty standup fight on our hands tonight."

"I'm going to send the sappers around to mine everyone's positions. As you retreat out of them, we'll blow them up once the demons have moved in."

"Djevels," Sean corrected.

"Ha, ha. Better warn the magic users to keep an eye on their ward."

"I'll do that," Sean said and tuned his radio to the frequency they used to contact the base. It took a few minutes to get Roxy on the line.

"What's up, Hon?"

"We're expecting a big push tonight. More likely than not, I'm sure some djevels are going to get by us."

"So you want me to alert the magic users to keep an eye on their ward?"

"Exactly. And if you can spare them a helicopter or two, send out a couple of the tracking teams."

"I'll call Clyde, the horse clan head, and let him know his people should expect to see a lot of activity tonight."

"How are they working out?" Sean said. "I'd all but forgotten about their offer to patrol the borders and help track any demon runners."

"So far they're working out great. The magic users love 'em because they're cautious and not overly gung-ho."

"Unlike the wolves?"

"The wolves, the boars, the cheetahs, the leopards, the tigers, and even a few lions I know!" Roxy chuckled. "So why are you so sure they're attacking tonight? From the reports I've been getting, it seems like it's been pretty dull out there."

"For exactly that reason."

"Okay, I'll let the airbase know they need to double their guard."

"Thanks, love you."

"Love you, too."

"That reminds me," Adam said as Sean hung up, "I better call Ryla."

"Afraid she'll be mad?"

Adam snorted. "I know you two don't get along, Sean, but the truth is, I really do love her."

"Well, good for you. Go call her, I'll go look for those sappers Chad's sending us."

The sappers showed up just as the sun was setting, and Sean spent the next hour helping them get the mines and the claymores set up, with Hunter's help. They then went off to help the next group over, as Sean and the rest settled in to wait.

"How long until the attack?" Adam asked.

"Oh, I'd give it another hour," Hunter said from where he was watching the gateway.

"Why's that?"

"Because they're coming out of the gateway pretty fast and building up their numbers."

Swearing, Sean and Adam picked up their binoculars and started looking.

"Chad, are you seeing what I'm seeing?" Sean called over the radio.

"Yup. As soon as the sappers are done, I'm going to send up a flare, and we'll start opening up with the heavy weapons. I just don't want them attacking us until we've got our defenses finished."

"Well, at least tell the snipers to start picking off the leaders."

"Will do!"

Sean got his own rifle and started looking for targets of opportunity as well. He'd hit his third one when suddenly a bunch of flares went up, and the battle was on. The djevels attacked almost immediately; most of them were bonde and gnashers with råges driving them on, marching out of their fort and coming around the berms.

It started off as a slaughter—there were a *lot* of defenders, and they all had rifles with iron bullets—but the attackers broke into a run, and for all that they kept falling, more and more of them kept coming.

"Grenades!" Sean called out as he swapped magazines and continued firing. The djevels were getting closer and closer with each wave.

"You know, maybe we should have attacked them before they got so many through this time," Adam growled as his rifle jammed and he quickly cleared it.

"I know, right?" Sean growled back.

"Everyone! Fall back!" Sean called and, casting a flame jet, he swept it back and forth in front of the demons that had now advanced to within twenty feet. The moment everyone had jumped up out of the trenches, the first row of claymores went off, devastating the front rows, giving Sean and the others enough time to run down the rise to their next defensive position, which was already manned by a large group of reserves.

Taking a moment to refresh their supplies of ammunition, Sean took a breather and looked at the men around him. There were a lot of black jaguars there, and the rest were mostly tigers and bears.

"Well, as I live and breathe, Gunny Wyatt! Nice to see you all made your hybrid forms."

"It's an ill wind that blows no good, Sir."

Sean snorted. "Call me Sean. Save the 'sir' bit for the officers."

Just then the mines that had been laid down in the trenches up above went off, killing the next wave of attackers.

"Well, time to get back to work," Sean said, raising his rifle and shooting at the next wave, which was stumbling over the trenches up above.

"You're not holding any grudges, are you, Sean?" Wyatt asked in a voice loud enough to be heard over the gunfire.

"Not against you or yours, Wyatt. We're good," he replied, equally loud. Sean had noticed that a lot of the men around him had been paying close attention to what he was saying between shots.

"But these djevel bastards? Oh yeah, I want them all dead!"

"Well, I think we can help you with that, right boys?"

Sean was surprised at the sudden loud calls of 'Hoorah!' followed by a bunch of very loud barks.

The fighting increased in tempo then, as more and more of the demons came over the hill and down towards them. The groups on their flanks had started firing into the demons as well.

"Chad!" Sean called over the radio. "Do you want us to fall back slowly or counterattack?"

"Fall back! They're trying to break out on your position! I've got help coming, but don't try to stand your ground until I tell you to!"

"Got it! Everyone!" Sean raised his voice. "We're going to pull back slowly and draw them out! Slowly!"

Sean started to retreat, slinging his rifle and drawing his sword. This was going to get nasty.

When the leading line of bonde reached him, Sean started in with his sword and was surprised to see the Marines had affixed their bayonets and were using them quite effectively. Apparently the dwarves had turned out a large supply of faerie bayonets, and the Marines seemed to be quite adept at switching from stabbing to shooting and back again.

The men of Hunter's squad were still using their rifles, but they were using the Marines as cover, shooting over or around them into the attackers. It was a tactic that was actually working fairly well. Adam had drawn his sword now, as well, and was mirroring Sean's tactics about twenty feet down the line to his right.

It was some eternity later, Sean had lost all track of time, when yet another couple of larger demons started drawing near. It soon became clear that it was the usual pair of a ridder and a biskop, but this time there was only the one set. Sean and the others had killed quite a few of these tonight. This pair had a large number of gnashers surrounding them, which made Sean wonder if perhaps they were running out of the bonde?

The fight got more vicious then, as it became clear that this was about as far as they could go. Sean stopped retreating at that point and waved his sword, almost too tired to yell for the others to halt. But they noticed he'd stopped, and immediately followed suit. Grunting, Sean kicked the bonde in front of him, and moved forward once more. Checking his mana level, he saw there was no way he could use any spells at this point. He'd taken so many hits that he needed all his power simply to stay alive and keep healing his wounds.

But man was he *tired.*

The jag fighting next to him he didn't recognize. Same for the werewolf on his other side. Wyatt had switched out with someone else a while ago, probably to get some rest, and that one had left…well, Sean couldn't remember when. The only thing keeping him going at this point was a need to be seen rallying the troops, and he suspected some sort of power from the energy all lions got from the lycans around them.

Risking a glance at Adam, he could see Adam looked just as exhausted as he did, but was also fighting on.

"You need to take a break, Adam," Sean gasped over the radio.

"Speak for yourself, I ain't letting some kid show me up in front of all these people."

"How about you *both* take a break before I call your wives and have your asses handed to you?" Chad called over the radio. "Seriously, we've got a handle on this, let the others hold them off for a while."

"Does he always play this dirty?" Adam gasped.

"No, sometimes he gets *mean*," Sean replied and, waving the others forward, he took a step back from the line. Another soldier, this one a bear, quickly stepped up and filled in the gap.

Sean just stood there, panting and watching for a while, as they slowly, inch by inch, started to push the demons back. After a few minutes, someone came up and took a hold of his arm.

"Come on, you look like you need a break."

Turning, Sean saw it was one of the jaguar Marines.

"Yeah, a break would be good," Sean said slowly. He noticed Adam was stumbling back as well. "Someone better help Adam before he falls over."

Sean keyed his radio as he was led over to a place to sit down and catch his breath. "What's the word, Chad?"

"Once the sun comes up, we'll start shelling them again. Yours wasn't the only spot they tried to break out, but it was probably the largest."

"How long until that happens?"

"Twenty minutes. Haven't you noticed how bright it's getting?

"Not really, no. How many of them got away?"

"Fifty? A hundred? More, maybe? Some of them slipped through the lines and managed to keep going because they didn't stop to fight anybody."

"And no one killed them?"

"We got stretched pretty thin in a few places."

"Yeah, well, I'm feeling pretty stretched myself right now. I lost count of how many bonde, råge, ridder, and biskops I killed last night."

"Yeah, you and Adam put on a strong showing, alright."

"It's a lion thing," Adam interrupted over the radio.

"You guys say that a lot, don't you?"

"Yeah," Sean laughed. "It's a lion thing. How much longer until the gateway closes?"

"Eighteen hours."

"Great, a bite to eat, something to drink, and we can go kill some more."

"They've stopped reinforcing and have actually started retreating. They shot their wad; I don't think they're looking to sacrifice anymore than they have to at this point."

"Well, if you say so," Sean said. Looking around at the soldiers resting on the ground, he asked one of them, "Is there anything to drink around here? Maybe something to eat?"

"Yeah, a beer would really hit the spot right now," Adam said, stretching out a few feet away. "Wake me when they get here."

"You guys want to go back in there, to that?" One of the tigers asked, pointing at the fight. "You've been there for like ten hours!"

"All part of the service," Adam muttered closing his eyes. "All part of the service."

Ξ

King Sladd strode into the room. Stopping just inside, he looked around and surveyed all who were waiting to attend him. His princes were all prostrate before his throne, as the law decreed.

Arrayed behind them were their assorted hangers-on. Advisors, playthings, whatever. Leaving a member of your entourage unattended in Sladd's castle was never a wise idea. Sladd was not adverse to taking those found alone and unattended and eating them. Finding a good meal was rather difficult in the times between passes, after all.

Continuing on to his throne, he sat and took another look around the room.

"Rise," he commanded, and his princes, all six of them, did just that.

"So tell me, Prince Talt, what happened?"

"We were repulsed again, Your Majesty."

Sladd smiled; he liked to make them admit before the others when they'd failed. He'd been letting each of them take a chance at the storsindet gates as they opened. It was too bad one of the hellige gates for the storsindets had been destroyed; King Sladd often wondered what that idiot Ansigt had done to cause it. Up until then, he'd been willing to look the other way as Ansigt had played his little games, thinking if he ended up with a seventh prince his power would grow so great that he might take on a lesser king and possess his princes, as well.

"Is that all?" King Sladd asked, his thoughts returning to the matter at hand.

"No, Your Majesty. I now believe that it would be possible to build and maintain a fort under the new attacks the lions have been using against us. Their weapons are less effective at night. So if we were to bring our mages out to construct shields during that time, we could construct a fort from which to sally forth and destroy our enemy."

Sladd nodded. "What else?"

"The hosts of the lions are most tenacious this time around. They were able to put up a surprising amount of resistance. It will be a week before I can report for certain how many got past them and out into the fruitful plains of our sacred hunting grounds."

Sladd looked a little surprised at that. "Didn't you tell them to contact you?"

Prince Talt shook his head. "Not for a short span of days, Your Majesty. I have been concerned about the mages with whom the lions have made an allegiance. I did not want those who got past their defenses to do anything that might expose them until they are well and far away."

"Ah," King Sladd said and nodded. This was why Prince Talt was the first among his princes. He was smarter than most, and craftier than all. Times like this made King Sladd wonder if perhaps the time to replace Prince Talt may be coming near. Sooner or later, he would try to replace Sladd and crown himself king. It was the way of things. That was how Sladd had risen to power so many hundreds of passes ago.

He suspected the only thing really holding Talt back at this point was the other princes. Because when a new king rose from the princely circle, the first thing he did was to kill all the other princes. The lords and the rest would be so busy scrambling for the open positions, it would give the new king time to secure his position and forge new alliances with the new emerging princes.

"Well then, let us discuss what our strategy will be for the next storsindet gate. Prince Skarm, I believe it will be your turn?"

"Thank you, Your Majesty," Prince Skarm said, and then proceeded to outline his own plans for the next gateway. Apparently his sole goal would be to plant a large number of demon eggs in an attempt to sow discord when they hatched. Which would be weeks after the gate had closed and, hopefully, all enemy activity had left the area.

King Sladd found it a novel plan. Oh, there would be breakout attempts and other things, but those were just to distract from the main plan. Though they wouldn't hesitate to take advantage of anything they might find.

When Prince Skarm had finished, he dismissed them all, paying extra attention to Prince Talt as he left the room. Once they were all gone, he went to talk to his own advisors, who had been spying on the meeting from the next room. After that, he would talk with the spies he had planted in several of the princes' entourages.

Preparation and Discovery

Geoffrey stood in the parking lot with Pastor Cross, George, and Cheranko, looking at the two trucks.

"There's no way you're going to get that tanker truck up the hill without them stopping you," George said to Geoffrey.

"I've been thinking about that," George said. "They have a lot of helicopters up there, right?"

Geoffrey and the others nodded. "What of it?"

"Helicopters need gas, or jet fuel, or something like that. I bet they have tanker trucks going up there all the time."

"So you think they won't notice one more?" Geoffrey asked, still a little skeptical.

"Not if we paint it to look like the other ones. I mean, who's going to want to bother looking at 'yet another tanker truck', right?"

"And we should paint the other one to look like a UPS truck!" Cheranko said excitedly.

"UPS? Why UPS?" Pastor Cross asked looking at him.

"Because they're everywhere! Who notices them? Have you ever looked at one and asked 'what's he doing here?' No! Because they're everywhere. You never think twice about it."

Geoffrey laughed. "Too bad we can't do that with a tanker truck! 'Cause he's right. They're everywhere, and you never think twice when you see one! Good call, Cheranko!"

Cheranko smiled at the praise from Geoffrey as Pastor Cross and George both nodded in agreement. Pastor Cross couldn't help but notice just how pleased Cheranko looked with himself. Geoffrey was right; it wouldn't take much to convince the young man that this was what he needed to do.

"How are we going to hold the stuff in the truck?" George asked. "It's empty back there."

"One of those big plastic water tanks from the farm goods store should handle it," Cheranko suggested again.

"Damn, I'm sure glad you're on our side!" George laughed and clapped him on the back. "I was thinking we'd just build something, but I like your idea better."

"Me too," Pastor Cross said with a smile. "I think the Lord gifted us all when he sent you to us, young man! You've just saved us a lot of time, and a lot of effort.

"Geoffrey, see if you can't find out what the tanker needs to look like. Cheranko, why don't you and George see if you can find one of those tanks that'll fit into the back of that truck. I'll see about getting it painted after you've picked that up."

"What about the," Geoffrey looked around, "stuff we need to put in them?"

"I'll be talking to our dear friends over at the ALS about that today," Pastor Cross said with a smile. "I think they said they'd have it in a few more days; they've already started preparing."

Pastor Cross gave Geoffrey the keys to the car he'd been using, then walked over to the small office they'd had to rent in order to get access to the large parking lot. He had to admit that Robert King was a most thorough man. Anything Cross had asked for, Mr. King had gotten for him almost immediately.

Going inside, he locked the door behind him. Picking up the old-fashioned phone that used an actual landline, he called Mr. King. Apparently the government couldn't tap phones like this without a warrant, unlike cellphones, which apparently were all tapped by some sort of national agency with 'super-computers' and such.

Pastor Cross briefly wondered if that should be his next campaign? Once the animals were dealt with, of course.

"Hello?" someone answered.

"Is Mr. King in? It's Pastor Cross."

"Just a moment."

It was only a few seconds before he heard Mr. King on the phone.

"Was your trip successful?" King asked him.

"Yes, we have what we need, and will have it ready to be used in a couple of days. What about our cargo?"

Mr. King had told Cross, while their phones shouldn't be tapped, it would be foolish to tempt fate, and they should be careful about what they said all the same.

"I'm afraid it's going to take us a bit longer to supply your needs, Pastor."

"What! Why? How much longer?"

"Well, you see, we're limited as to how much we can procure each day, and my teams are having to drive all over to find what they need. When it was only the cargo for the one, it was a simple task. But even you must admit that your wonderful idea is going to take a great deal more then we were first prepared to acquire."

Pastor Cross sighed. "Fine, but we can't wait too long. Send us whatever you have, as soon as you can, and we'll deal with it. The second has four sections; if we can fill three of those, I'll be pleased."

"We'll have the first shipment there by Friday. I'll call you, but the rest of it shouldn't be much longer than that."

"Thank you," Pastor Cross said and hung up.

#

Special Agent Dilardo was looking at the report his two analysts, Mary and Chester, had just given him.

"Okay, what am I looking at here?" he asked, looking at the two of them sitting across the desk from him. They were quite the unlikely pair. Mary looked like an underwear model, and often dressed as provocatively as she could. Chester looked like Clarke Kent, the ultimate clueless straight man, right down to the suit and tie.

"We're seeing a large upswing in fertilizer sales in California, Oregon, Southern Nevada, and Utah," Mary said.

"Define large?"

"Enough so far to fill a large box truck to the top," Chester said.

"It's probably just some farmers. Have you called the stores?"

Mary nodded. "Yes, we called several of them. They've all reported a ten percent increase in bag sales."

"We only noticed," Chester continued, "because the manufacturer called us to report an unexpected increase in product sales."

"They called you?" Dilardo asked.

"It's required," Mary said.

"By law," Chester agreed.

Dilardo sighed and looked at the report; there were a number of charts and maps in it, probably

Mary's work. She was good at putting information into easy to digest pictures. Chester tended to stick to the legal and statistical aspects. Paging through it some more, he came to a map of the western states, and sure enough, Mary had color coded it to show where the increase in sales were. The pattern there was quite interesting.

"Do you think you could add some time stamps to this graphic?" Dilardo asked.

Mary leaned over the desk, reminding Dilardo once again of her unofficial office nickname, the one human resources would have a fit over if they knew, and turned a few pages.

"There."

Dilardo looked it over and nodded. "Okay, thanks. I'll have the teams call the rental agencies and keep their eyes open for anything suspicious.

"I think this level of planning indicates that we're not dealing with some homegrown terrorists, Sir," Chester said.

"They're all homegrown, Chester," Dilardo said with a smile. "Some are just more capable than others. Is there anything else you two have for me? I'd say from what you've shown me here, the chances are high that somebody is planning something. But we're still left without a target."

"The target is inside the circle, Sir," Mary said.

"The probabilities suggest it to be almost a certainty." Chester agreed.

"And how many square miles are inside that circle?" Dilardo asked. "How many towns? Cities? Keep me apprised of the situation, but I don't think we have anything to worry about just yet. If I show this to my boss, they're going to want answers. Answers we don't have."

Mary sighed rather dramatically, causing her shirt to stretch in a most distracting fashion.

"Yes, Sir."

"I still think you're making a mistake, Sir," Chester added, "but I see your point. Come M, let's see if we can't find something more definitive."

"Okay, C."

Special Agent Dilardo shook his head quietly as they left his office. They really were a good team. But they were also complete nerds who believed that everything was a conspiracy. Two years ago they'd tried to sell him on some secret conspiracy that had been going on for decades, perhaps centuries, after a couple of terrorist attacks in Sparks. Thank god he'd sat on those! He could just imagine what the response would have been.

He left the report sitting in his 'priority' box. He'd pass their information around the office and see if anyone could turn it into a lead, but more likely it was that kid in Reno buying up everything he could get his hands on. Dilardo had heard through channels that the kid liked to blow things up, and the government was more than willing to look the other way.

#

Meanwhile on the other side of town, Steve looked at the troops Sean had sent him. He'd arranged for fifty to bunk over at Sapientia, and another fifty over at Eruditio. Both had agreed that Sean's concerns were valid and welcomed the extra protection, especially as they didn't have to pay the upkeep for them.

To Steve, it meant that once he sent these people out, he'd have two more secure facilities he could stage his events from, even if the ALS managed to tie him down at their main building. Two more groups of people their German spies didn't have pictures of.

"Okay everyone," he said, looking around the hanger. They'd all just gotten off the airliner Sean had chartered to bring them here. He didn't want to give any of the spies out there a chance to learn how many reinforcements they'd gotten.

"As you've no doubt been told before you were sent here, things are starting to ramp up in the DC area. Mostly it's the ALS freaks, so we're going to target them first. But there's a distinct chance we may come under a more direct attack from other forces, and that 'we' includes Sapientia and Eruditio, who are both our known allies.

"What this means is, I'm going to need fifty of you to go to their compounds when you leave here and hook up with their existing security, so if things do go sideways, they won't have to wait for us to send reinforcements. Because you'll already be there."

"So we're back to protecting the magic users?" someone asked in the ranks.

"Only of they're attacked," Steve said, and then smiled. "The *real* reason we're putting you there is so the people who are spying on us won't know you're here. You're going to be a third of our forces in the area, and yes, do I have plans for you!

"You see, right now they've got us under heavy surveillance, and breaking free from that is a difficult job with the small numbers we have. Even doubling the people at our headquarters, they still have a lot more resources. But if they don't know about you…"

"They can't follow us!" someone said with a laugh.

Steve nodded. "Exactly. Now, here's what we're going to do. Right now the ALS people are doing all sorts of protests, propaganda ads, events, you name it. All to make us look bad. They're provoking us constantly, trying to get us to throw the first punch, because whoever breaks first is going to get a lot of bad PR."

"So you want us to attack them anonymously?"

Steve recognized the wolf talking; it was Ogg, one of the ones Sean had captured from the Vestibulum.

"No, we want them to attack *us*! In public, and with *lots* and *lots* of witnesses, too!"

"And just how does that happen?" Ogg asked, looking confused.

Steve smiled widely. "Simple! We're going to have those of you who are staying at the magic users' compounds infiltrate the ALS movement. You'll show up at their protests and join the crowd. We'll even see about getting the mages to put illusions on some of you to look like some of the more recognizable ALS members."

"Oh!" Ogg said with a sudden smile. "I get it! We'll 'attack' the lycans they're harassing, so the ALS gets the blame!"

"Exactly," Steve said, grinning. "One or two of you will lead the attack; the rest will try to egg on the rest of the protesters to see if we can get some of them to attack as well. By the time the police act, the ones who actually started the attack will be long gone, and only the real protesters will be left."

"Won't that look suspicious if the attackers take flight like that?" asked Card, the surviving prime who had signed up with Sean, and who, due to his experience, was now leading one of the ten wolf teams.

"Yes, it will look very suspicious. It'll make it clear that the ALS has decided to up the ante by using physical attacks, while making sure the perpetrators avoid arrest. Though if you can get away without being seen, all the better."

"So when do we start?"

"As soon as you get settled in. Granite and Tisha will circulate among you in a minute so we can decide who will be best, where. We also have a few simple rules about these attacks that I want to be sure you all understand before we leave here. Mostly they're covert identifiers so you'll know who in a group to attack. The attacks will start out as minor things at first, thrown liquids in faces, that kind of thing. But we'll be ramping it up eventually to physical attacks, once we're sure the groundwork has been laid."

"Sounds painful," Card said with a grimace.

"I'm sure it will be; that's why I've agreed to be one of the targets, once it gets that far," Steve told them. "We're running a false flag operation here, we need to push it over the top, and you all need to remember, we don't talk about this with anyone in public, not even each other.

"Now, let's get you all sorted out. We can supply the rest of the details later," Steve said, stepping down and finishing as Granite and Tisha gathered up the team alphas to find out who would be best for the different positions.

"Do you really think this will work?" Nate asked Steve.

"When it comes to the news, 'if it bleeds, it leads'. Oh yeah, this is going to work. Tisha is going to order them not to talk to anyone about this without permission, so we don't have to worry about loose lips. The ALS people have already tried to kill me once, no one is going to be surprised they'll try it a second time."

Thirty minutes later, Steve left with the hundred who were going to be his 'extra support'. The other hundred would wait a couple of hours before filtering out to the two magic user compounds, just in case any of the people watching Steve had managed to follow him to the airport.

"So how is this going to work?" Criss, one of the team alphas, asked Steve. They were all sitting around a conference table and had just finished settling in the new people. Steve, Terri, Tisha, Granite, Nate, and several of the other alphas from the teams had joined them.

Steve started off, "Most of our people are known to the Anti-Lycan Society. They've been taking pictures of everyone coming and going, all that stuff."

"But they don't know anything about the people we sent to the two councils, and the magic users are a lot more secretive, as well as pro-active about their secrecy," Terri added. "So while they know about those of us who have been here, and will be learning about the new ones, they don't know anything about them."

"Okay, so?" Criss said

Steve picked it back up. "So when they spot some of our better known people, the ones we know they have records on, it's not going to surprise anybody when they harass them, right?"

"They're doing that already!" Nate grumbled. "I can't go food shopping without someone creating a scene!"

"Right, so we're going to have our unknown friends infiltrate those groups, and they're going to know when and where you're going to be, because we're going to tell them."

"As if my life wasn't miserable enough."

Terri laughed and the others all smirked. "Oh, it's going to get a lot worse."

"How so?"

"We're going to have them start throwing stuff at you. We'll start off with sodas, milk shakes, things that cause a mess, but won't hurt anybody."

"Can I hit them?" Kyle, one of the other alphas, asked hopefully.

"No, no one is going to be hitting anybody. For the next few weeks, we're all going to get harassed. Things will be thrown at us—feel free to dodge by the way—and our cars will get scratched and vandalized. The goal is to create an atmosphere of violence."

"The police never do anything about this kind of shit," Granite said. "They mostly can't be bothered. Technically it's assault, but they don't want to waste their time on something that no one ever gets convicted or even fined for."

"And," Steve said, continuing, "it almost always leads to a ramping up of violent behavior."

"Which I take it is part of the plan?" Criss asked.

Steve nodded. "We'll wait a few weeks, then we'll start off with some simple assaults. Their leadership will probably try to nip it in the bud…"

"If they're smart," Terri interjected.

"…but as it's our people doing it, they're not going to have much success, and the rank and file will see that as either a loss of control, or just lip service to avoid lawsuits, believing the leadership is actually behind all of it."

"The big thing is," Terri told her, " these people are always angry, and they're always looking for an excuse, a victim to victimize. So we're hoping they start getting violent without our help once we've primed the pump."

"Why?"

"So they get arrested, and we get some nice news articles," Steve said with a grin. "John Q. Public is not going to take very well to seeing a bunch of stupid college kids assaulting innocent people who are minding their own business."

"Assuming they take our side."

"Oh, they will," Steve said with a glint in his eye. "Because *I* have a cunning and brilliant plan."

"You know that never worked, right?"

"Actually, it worked once, and in this case, once will be all we'll need."

#

Karl sat in the car while Otto and Raban carefully approached the old abandoned bunker. They'd spent several days checking every abandoned building Karl remembered, as well as a few he didn't, but which there were records on back at the office. Otto had been the one to remember the old bunker. Karl had forgotten about it as well. It was far out from any of the towns or villages, now well hidden by a couple of copses of trees that had grown up around it.

When Karl was a child, there had been dozens of them scattered all over the countryside, though mainly in or around the towns. Removing them was a major undertaking; they'd been built to withstand bombs during the war, after all. So this one, out in the country, wasn't worth the money to demolish, and had instead been left out here to rot.

Kids still came out here, either on dares, or to get drunk or stoned. But few officers bothered coming here because it was so far out of town.

Karl looked down at the AK-47 sitting in his lap, loaded, with the safety off. Both Otto and that Raban fellow were armed with them, as well. It was illegal, of course, and the guns were probably black market, but over the last few days, Karl was gaining a newfound respect for the phrase 'keep your mouth shut'.

With the removal of most of the people from town, the demons had gone on to attack the neighboring village last night. Hannah had been ordered over there early this morning to take control of things. She'd told Karl she doubted she'd be back, and the investigation into the deaths here had all been ordered closed.

It was the first time he'd seen her look truly worried. The order to close the cases had come from Berlin, and she'd admitted to him before she left that it was highly unusual.

The sound of automatic gunfire woke him quite suddenly from his reverie. Starting the car, he put it in reverse and began to back up, quickly making a three-point turn as the gun shots continued, followed by a couple of small explosions.

Looking in his mirror, he started to drive away slowly. Raban had been clear that he needed to run away, but Karl was still loath to leave them behind.

Looking up from the mirror, he saw it. It was black as printer's ink, and wearing what he could only describe as tattered, rotting skins. It looked at him and screamed in a voice that reminded Karl of a hundred fingernails being dragged across a chalkboard. It then pointed at him and screamed again, a confused looking coming over its face.

It looked even more confused when Karl, flooring the accelerator, hit it and ran it over. Then, jamming the car into reverse, he ran it over a second time for good luck.

"Get out of here!" Otto said, diving into the back seat. Karl noticed he no longer had his rifle, and his clothing was torn.

"What about your friend?"

"Go!" Otto yelled.

Karl floored it, the car bouncing over the old dirt road that led from the hidden ruins. He saw it then, a lion running flat out, with several black shapes giving chase.

Otto reached over the seat, grabbed the rifle, and fired bursts at the things chasing Raban, dropping several and causing the rest to slow. Easing back on the throttle, Karl moved his eyes between Raban, the things chasing him, and the road ahead.

"In front of us!" Otto yelled as several more of those disturbing looking *things* popped up.

The windshield suddenly exploded as Otto shot through it, dropping two of them as Karl ran over yet another one.

He heard more shattering glass then, and looking back, he saw that Raban had jumped through the window—or tried to, at least. He'd shifted back to his human form and was half inside, half outside. Otto had grabbed him and was trying to pull him into the back of the car.

Karl floored it again, and this time he didn't slow down for anything or look anywhere but straight ahead. When they hit the pavement, the car lurched around a bit, tires squealing, before they bit and the car rocketed off down the lane towards the highway.

"You can slow down now!" Raban yelled.

"What?" Karl yelled back. His ears were still ringing from the gunfire in the enclosed space, and the wind blowing through the ruined windshield at a hundred and forty kilometers per hour.

"Slow Down!" Raban yelled again.

"Is it safe?" Karl asked as he let the car slow to a more sedate pace of a hundred kilometers an hour.

"I think so. We lost them, at any rate."

"How many were there?"

"At least thirty, possibly more," Otto said.

"We could have gotten them all if we'd been better prepared," Raban grumbled.

"There were too many of them for just the two of us," Otto retorted. "At least we killed half of them."

Raban sighed. "I guess you're right. Still, the First isn't going to be pleased."

"Who's that?" Karl asked.

"The head lion," Otto told him. "And I guess Raban's charm worked."

"Why's that?"

"'Cause you're still here. That first one you ran over? He was trying to rip your soul out."

Karl blinked and slammed on the brakes, hard.

"What the hell?" Raban growled as he slammed into the back of the front seat.

"I…I don't feel very well…" Karl said. Opening the door, he got out of the car, stumbled over to the side, and threw up. He could hear Raban and Otto talking back in the car.

"You sure about what you saw?" Raban was quizzing Otto.

"I think so. It pointed at him and was yelling something. Why? What was that charm?"

"Protection against mind spells. We use them as protection from the magic users. Guess they work against devils, too."

"Luckily for Karl."

"You done out there?" Raban called out.

Standing up straight, Karl got out a handkerchief and wiped his mouth, then slowly made his way back to the idling car. Getting in, he put on his seatbelt, closed the door, and started driving back to town again.

"I'd throw both of your asses out of town if I thought it would make the slightest bit of difference." Karl sighed. "I want my old life back."

Otto snorted. "You and me both."

"I'm driving back to my house. I'll leave you the car; I don't care where you go."

"What are you going to do?"

"I hear Italy's nice this time of year,"

"What about the rest of the townspeople?"

"The hell with them," Karl said, frowning. "I warned them all to go. Any who are left, well, they're no longer my concern. In fact, I think I'll be quitting my job here once I'm far enough away they can't stop me."

Otto looked over at Raban. "I just might join you."

Napalm Love

"It's been two days," Mary griped.

"I hear you, M," Chester agreed.

"So what do we do about it, C?" she asked him.

"I was thinking we should call somebody."

"We call anybody, and they'll just sit on it like de-*lard*-oh-butt has been," she grumbled.

"Only if we call somebody in the agency," he pointed out.

"But who else in Homeland would even be interested? This whole thing points to Nevada more and more, every day now!"

Chester smiled. "What if we called the governor's office?"

Mary laughed. "You know they'll try to fire us both for that!"

"Admit to nothing!" Chester grinned.

"Blame everything!" Mary agreed with a smile of her own.

"Shall we?"

"Of course! Milk and Cheese are innocent!" she said, referring to their two 'unofficial' nicknames, adopted when they'd both discovered their mutual fondness for a certain comic strip some years ago after meeting up at work. Of course the people at work had all picked up on it, though they thought the 'Milk' name was due to her large chest, and Chester's 'Cheese' name had something to do with a certain advertising mascot.

"Well, break out the gin; we got some phone calls to make."

"Hello, this is Chester Boneillo with the FBI..."

"Hi, this is Special Agent Mary Catalano from the FBI…"

"Special Agent Boneillo here…"

"What do you mean this isn't something you can deal with? Aren't you in charge…"

"I appreciate your concerns, but yes I'm legitimate. Call the FBI's main office and ask to speak to me!" Chester sighed and slammed the phone down.

"You know what? I want to speak to the governor! No, not his secretary, the man himself! I'm quite tired of you running me around. We're the ever-loving FBI! You *may* have heard of us? We had a TV show once? Oh good, yes, that's us! Now put me through, or I swear I'm gonna set the entire Reno office outside your home for the next month!"

Mary turned to Chester. "I think I got a live one, pick up on the line over there and listen in."

"Of course I'll hold," Mary said into the phone. "Just understand that if we have to waste time flying out there, I will *personally* make you regret it!"

"Okay, okay already," Chester heard from the other side of the conversation as he put the phone to his ear. "You don't have to bite my head off!"

"We're sorry," Chester said then, "but we've been trying to get through for over an hour now, and for some odd reason, no one wants to talk to us."

"Okay, I'm putting you through to the governor's office."

The line clicked, and then someone picked up."

"Governor's office, how may I help you?" a woman's voice said.

Mary sighed heavily, great, *another* roadblock.

"This is special agent Chester Boneillo from the FBI, we've been tracking data on explosive sales, and we have reason to believe that a group of terrorists are targeting Reno."

"One moment, let me put you through to the task force."

"You have a task force?" Mary said surprised.

"All that stuff on the news ain't a fairy tale," she said, and the phone clicked again.

"Governor's taskforce on terror, Trooper Barrett speaking, how can I help you?"

"Thank god! Finally!" Mary said. "This is Mary Catalano, Federal Bureau of Investigation, and we have reason to believe that someone is about to hit you with a very large truck bomb."

"Oh? Based on what?"

"Fertilizer sales. You got an email address? I can send you the report right now."

"Sure," Trooper Barrett replied and gave it to her. It only took a moment to send him the presentation with all of the files.

"Great! Got it…let's see…" There was a very lengthy pause.

"Are you still there?" Mary asked after a minute.

"You know what, give me your phone number. Catalano, you said? I need to show this to my boss. I don't think it's that guy up north."

Several minutes later Mary hung up the phone and high-fived Chester.

"Success!"

"Now let's get out of here before they fire us!" Chester said with a grin.

"Onward, to mayhem!" Mary agreed.

#

Geoffrey sat down at the far end of the bar away from everyone else. It was after nine, going on ten. He didn't have to be at the yard where they were fueling up the tanker and the other truck until midnight. He'd been a little annoyed at how long it took them to get all the fertilizer; apparently buying that much in one place would get the feds on your ass in a heartbeat these days. So some of Pastor Cross's 'friends' from the ALS had set up a buying operation, where they'd go from place to place and buy a few bags at each one. Yeah, it had taken them almost two weeks, but they got it all here, and nobody was the wiser.

They'd had to steal a tanker truck full of diesel, but hand a driver enough cash, and more than a few of them were willing to look the other way.

All he knew was, the waiting had been rough. It had burned at him, eating away at his courage. But he'd given his word, and he knew it was the right thing to do, because he'd made Pastor Cross so happy. So he figured a little bit of liquid courage wouldn't hurt him.

It's not like he'd have to worry about falling off the wagon ever again, after tonight.

"Geoffrey! What are you doing in here? I thought you quit drinking!"

Turning to look, he saw Roy Baum, one of the ones who'd quit after they were let out of jail.

"Traitor," Geoffrey grunted and turned back to the bartender. "Jack, straight up."

"You got it," the bartender said and set up the drink as Roy came over and took the stool next to his.

"Go away, Roy." Geoffrey sighed.

"Can't, I work here," Roy said with a grin. "Got a job as a barback so I can cover the rent and food for me and Cindy. Seeing as we can't leave town until after the trial and all that."

"Then maybe I should be going..." Geoffrey said and started to stand.

Roy put his hand on Geoffrey's shoulder and pushed him back down.

"No, stay a few. I'll even pay for your drink."

"I don't really want to talk to you, Roy. You walked out and left us. You let your woman sway you against Cross."

Roy smiled, and Geoffrey noticed it wasn't a friendly smile, either.

"Oh, you don't have to do any talking, Geoff. I think I'll talk, and you can just listen. You're really good at that. I mean, you've been listening to Cross now for how long?

"By the way, Cindy's expecting. I'm finally gonna be a dad!"

Geoffrey frowned. "I thought you two couldn't have children?"

Roy nodded. "That's right, we can't. Wonder how that happened, right? Well," Roy paused and gave a small laugh. "*I* don't wonder; I know after all. But I can bet you're wondering. You're probably thinking 'that old Roy is just a broken-down steer, he can't knock up his wife! So who did?"

"I don't care if you and your slut wife are expecting." Geoffrey growled.

Roy laughed again. "You know, time was I would have put you through a wall for saying that. But I've learned there are meaner things you can do to a man. And if ever there was a man who needed it done to him, it's you, Geoff. It's *all* you!

"So, I hear your hot little daughter moved in with those animals up at that lion's compound?"

"You little..."

"Uh-uh! You're out on bail, Mr. Straight-and-Narrow! Throw one punch, and you'll be back in the slammer before the end of my shift. And I'm sure your good ole buddy 'Pastor Cross' wouldn't take kindly to hearing his number one man fell off the wagon and got into a bar fight, now would he?"

Geoffrey slowly uncurled his fingers from the fist he'd formed and put his hand back down on the bar.

"Drink your drink," Roy said nodding at it. "I'm not done yet. Know why your daughter moved up there?"

Geoffrey glanced at him, picked up his drink, and tossed the whole thing off in a gulp, then started to stand.

"Oh no, we're just getting started," Roy said and put his hand on Geoffrey's shoulder, pushing him back down.

"Timmy! Another round for my friend here!"

"Sure thing, Roy."

"You can't keep me here," Geoffrey said in a low voice.

"Seeing as the bouncers are friends of mine, too, I'd say you're wrong there. Now, answer the question: know why your daughter ended up there?"

"Because they got their hands on her and corrupted her!" Geoffrey said angrily, glaring at Roy.

"No. It's because you kicked her out on the street. Left her with nothing. Not a damn thing. Why would you do such a thing to your own daughter, Geoff? Why?"

"None of your business!"

"Oh, no!" Roy said with a laugh. "It's completely my business! You're here, aren't you? Oh, god, man, you're so fucking *thick* you don't just need things spelled out for you, you need a fucking *map*!"

Geoffrey turned to face Roy and snarled, "It's because she started saying bad things about our pastor! Okay? She came in there and said all sorts of nasty and evil things about him! They corrupted her! They took my little girl away and turned her into a fucking tramp! Just like her mother!"

"There's two things wrong with that story, Geoff. The first is, any corrupting of your daughter started back at home in the good pastor's office. The second is, she wasn't telling you any lies."

Geoffrey swore and took a swing at Roy, who slipped off his stool and dodged. He'd have thrown a second one, but someone grabbed him from behind, stopping him.

"The good 'Pastor Cross' was sleeping with your daughter, Geoff!" Roy said softly. "He's also the one who knocked up my Cindy. Told her it was "God's will", and I couldn't give her the child she wanted, and we thought maybe it really was God's will.

"Then I found out he was sleeping with your then seventeen-year-old daughter, and any man's wife he could get into his bed."

"What! You're lying!"

"Your daughter wanted your approval so much, she let the man you admired woo her, court her, take her to bed. She didn't know about the others, but Cindy did. So did I. I didn't say anything because I thought Pastor Cross really was doing God's work.

"And then the son-of-a-bitch shot them all in the back so he could make good his own escape! You're a fool, Geoffrey! You're nothing but a God's damned fool! I can't blame you for following that glib-tongued devil, because he fooled me, too! But when the facts where laid at your feet, you still refused to see the truths the good Lord put right in front of your face!

"I may not be a clever man, Geoff, but even I ain't that stupid! Now get the hell out of here, and I pray to the good Lord that I *never* see your face again!"

Roy motioned to the man behind him, and Geoffrey finally felt the grip holding him back let go of him. Turning to the door, he stormed out, leaving the bar behind.

"Friend of yours?" asked Jason, the bouncer, while Timmy looked on.

"Yeah, we grew up together. He was the best man at my wedding. Known him for over thirty years."

"Wow, harsh, man. What'dya think he'll do?"

Roy sighed and shook his head. "Something epically stupid, I'm sure."

Geoffrey swore to himself as he stomped off down the street. That bastard! Saying those things to him! Saying those things about Pastor Cross!

But, but…Geoffrey shook his head. Roy had never lied to him, he'd been there for him every time he'd needed help. He'd even quit drinking when Geoffrey had found out he was an alcoholic.

Now this.

Now this.

Roy had warned him about his drinking. He'd warned him about Peg, his wife, back before he'd married her. But Cross? Cross had done so much for him! He'd made him feel whole again, made him feel like he mattered. He shook his head. Someone was lying to him, but Roy had *never* lied to him. What if he was right?

What if Cross *had* been sleeping with his daughter? What if he *had* shot her in the back, and what she'd said to him was true?

Stopping, he looked around and spied a bench. He sat down and tried to think about it. Who was telling the truth? Who was lying? And how could he figure it out? Because he had about two hours to discover the truth. After that, none of it would matter anymore.

#

"Sean, we've got a problem."

Sean looked up from his son Sean Jr. at Bill Channing, Roxy's father and Sean Junior's grandfather.

"What is it now?" Sean asked with a shake of his head.

"I got a call from my contact in the governor's office. The Feds are worried because someone bought up a couple of tons of fertilizer."

"So?"

"You mix it with diesel fuel, and it becomes a rather impressive bomb."

Sean closed his eyes and took a breath. "Let me guess, they bought it all here in Reno?"

"Actually, no. They bought it pretty much everywhere *but* here in Reno. That's why they think it's coming here."

"Huh? I don't follow."

"You can't buy large amounts of fertilizer anymore, not unless you have a farm or a license or something. The government tracks that stuff about the same way they track nukes. Well, they noticed the demand had suddenly skyrocketed, and when they finally tracked it down, they fingered Reno, because no one was buying large amounts of it here."

"So why didn't they call us?"

Bill shrugged. "Best I can figure is, the Feds tracking this didn't put two and two together. But they had to inform the governor and his task force."

"And they informed you."

Sean remembered all the stories about truck bombs he'd read about back in school.

"So how many truck bombs are we talking here?"

"Three? Four?" Bill shook his head. "I'm not really sure."

"You talked to Oak, Rox, and the dwarves yet about this?"

Bill shook his head. "No. I came to you first."

"Rox?" Sean asked raising his voice slightly. Roxy was in the dining room, talking with the rest of their wives.

"Not me, Sean, Dad! I'll call Oak right now."

He heard a muttered comment, then Daelyn's voice called out. "I'll call me Uncle right away and see if he knows!"

"I think we better put some guards down in the neighborhood and tell them to watch out for any trucks heading this way," Sean said.

"But how do you stop it? You can't shoot it, it might explode!" Roxy said, coming out of the dining room with a phone to her ear.

"I guess I'll go down there now and lay a sleep trap," Sean said, handing Sean Junior over to Bill. "Probably should get a bunch of sleep wands and parcel them out to the guards, as well. Even if it does go off at the bottom of the driveway, hopefully that's far enough away it won't hurt us up here."

"What's the rush? Why would anyone try to come up here at night?" Peg asked, sticking her head out of the dining room as well. "They'd stand out like a sore thumb! We don't get deliveries here at night!"

"Well, with that much explosives, do you really want to take a chance they'll wait until morning? They must think we'll let them in, or they wouldn't be trying it," Bill said as he played with his grandson.

"In that case, I think I'm going to make them start searching everyone at the bottom of the hill from now on," Roxy said, then repeated that over the phone to Oak.

"Well, I got work to do…" Sean said, heading for the door, then he suddenly stopped.

"What?" Roxy and Peg both asked together.

"Our building downtown! They could hit that easy!"

"They wouldn't have needed so much just to destroy that," Bill pointed out.

"Well, there's the casino, Claudia's place, Chad's place! Roxy, tell Oak to spin up a helicopter, then call everyone you can think of and warn them."

"What are you going to do?"

"I don't know, but there's gotta be something we can do."

"You know what?" Peg said, looking thoughtful. "If they can't see it, they can't attack it."

"What do you mean?"

"I mean I'm coming with you. You too, Jo!"

"Why me?" Jolene protested.

"Because you're our own little magical generator!" Peg said with a snicker.

"I better come, too," Roxy said.

"Why?"

"Because none of you have a lick of common sense?" she said, looking around the room.

#

Geoffrey looked at his watch; it was almost eleven. He'd have to head back soon. Looking around, he noticed he was just across the street from the hospital. The one his daughter had been at. He seemed to recall something about an unpaid bill or two, but he'd been ignoring it.

"Well, not like *I'm* gonna need the money anymore." He sighed to himself. Getting up, he walked across the street and in through the front doors.

"Can I help you, sir?" the security guard behind the receptionist's desk said.

"Yeah, I'm leaving town in a few hours, and I wanted to settle up my daughter's medical bill before I left."

"You'll have to come back during regular hours, sir. The billing department is closed."

"Oh, come on, there has to be *somebody* in the hospital that can run a credit card. I mean, you guys are open all the time, right?"

The guard looked at him, then sighed. "Try the emergency room. If they're not too busy, they might be able to help you out."

"Thanks," Geoffrey said and followed the signs into the emergency receiving area.

"Can I help you, sir?" a woman behind a counter asked.

"Yeah, I have to leave town for work, and I won't be back for a long time. So I wanted to settle up my daughter's medical bill before I left."

"Do you have some ID, sir?"

Geoffrey nodded, got out his driver's license, and passed it over to the woman. "My daughter's name is Betty."

The woman nodded and started typing, then stopped and looked at him, and then at the record again.

"It says here it's paid in full."

Geoffrey blinked. "What? How can that be? She called me and told me she was broke and couldn't pay for it!"

"How long ago was that?"

"Little over a week ago. I was out of town working."

"Well, it says here it was paid five days ago by a Stewart Reese?"

Geoffrey shook his head. "I don't know him. Well, thanks for looking it up for me."

"Not a problem, Sir. And my condolences on the baby."

Geoffrey stopped and slowly turned to the woman as he suddenly felt something like ice crawling through his veins. "It was the gunshot wound that cost her the child, right?"

"Yes, sir. There aren't any more details than that. I have a contact for the police if you wish to talk to them?"

Geoffrey shook his head. "Maybe later. Though I am curious about one thing?"

"Yes?"

"Did they list who the baby's father was?"

"Well, I probably shouldn't tell you, but you are her father. It's listed as one Cross Macrey."

Turning around, Geoffrey stormed out the door of the emergency room, his face turning a deep red as things suddenly added up. She had been pregnant, and she'd lost the baby. She hadn't been with anyone other than Pastor Cross, or he would have noticed it.

She hadn't lied to him.

Roy hadn't lied to him either.

Only one person had.

Geoffrey didn't like being lied to. He liked being played for a fool even less. He'd lost his wife, but that hadn't been his fault. Losing his daughter? Oh, that was his fault alright, but at least he wasn't the only one to blame. Someone else had led him into that, and for that, they were going to pay.

The problem was, how could he get him alone? And what would he do once he had?

Pastor Cross looked at his watch again, it was a quarter to twelve, and Geoffrey still hadn't shown up. It wasn't like the man to be late, and where would he find another to take his place with so little time left? They'd gone over the plan again and again. For this to happen now, this endangered everything.

Just then his phone rang. Pulling it out, he saw it was Geoffrey calling.

"Geoffrey! Where are you?" Pastor Cross demanded.

"I'm with my daughter! I found her! They…they did some bad things to her, Pastor. She's hurt!"

"What? What do you mean, you found her?"

"I found her downtown, they were, they were making her do things, for money. It wasn't pretty! But I got her out of there! She's with me! I got her a room in a hotel. Those bastards! Those fucking bastards! What they did to her, Pastor! The things they were going to do! I'm going to kill every one of those mother fucking animals!"

Pastor Cross had to hold the phone away from his ear. Geoffrey was livid! He'd seen the man angry before, but never like this!

"Well, come on down here then and let's do this! We've got the truck waiting for you, just like we planned. You can kill them all, Geoffrey! You can send them to hell like the Lord demands!"

"I...I...I want to Pastor, but I can't leave her alone here! Not all by herself!"

"I could send a couple of brothers to keep an eye on her; she'd be safe then, Geoffrey."

"No! I've seen how they look at her, you know how they are! And with the way she is right now? She's too vulnerable! I don't want any of them by her! Especially not alone with her!"

"Geoffrey, we've been planning this for weeks now! We have everything ready to go, and to go now! Can't you just lock the door?"

"And then what? I'm not coming back, Pastor!"

"Would it be okay if I looked in on her?" Pastor Cross asked cautiously.

There was a moment's pause.

"She says she's okay with you, that she misses you, Pastor. But I don't want to leave her alone, not for a moment. I'm, I'm too worried about her."

Pastor Cross's eyes widened just a hair. She missed him? Then again, why wouldn't she? He had always treated her well, unlike those damn animals, apparently. He smiled a little to himself then. If she was as vulnerable as Geoffrey was claiming, maybe he wouldn't have to celebrate his greatest success alone tonight after all!

"I don't know, Geoffrey," he said, sounding a little uncertain. It wouldn't do to make Geoffrey think getting his hot little girl in a room alone was exactly what Cross wanted right now. "I mean, I could come right after you left, but everyone is ready to go here."

"Don't worry, Pastor, I know the plan as well as you do. I can leave to take care of everything as soon as you get here. Just tell them all to wait for me. We can leave an hour later; it won't cause any problems."

Pastor Cross gave a faked sigh. "Okay, Geoffrey. But only because it's you asking. I know I can trust you. Tell me where you are, and I'll be there as soon as I can. I wouldn't do this for anyone else."

Pastor Cross fidgeted a little in the elevator as went up in the tower. He was looking forward to getting his hands on little Betty once again. She'd been quite the little firecracker. Oh, not as experienced as some of the older women had been; Cindy had been quite the animal in bed. But Betty had shown a lot of promise, and with her father out of the way here shortly, there wouldn't be anyone to stop him from training her just they way he liked them.

He wondered if he'd be able to hear the explosions from inside the hotel? Geoffrey had gotten her a room fairly high up; no doubt he'd he able to see the one in town from this very tower.

The elevator dinged, and Pastor Cross got out and headed down the hallway to the room. He knocked on the door once, and it was immediately flung open by Geoffrey, who looked up and down the hallway.

"You didn't bring anyone else, did you?"

"Of course not, Geoffrey! I'm a man of my word. Clark is waiting in the car down by the lobby to drive you back, but that's it."

"Good!" Geoffrey said, grabbed Pastor Cross's arm, and pulled him inside the room, slamming the door behind him.

Pastor Cross stumbled, then looked around.

"Where is…" was all he got out of his mouth before he felt something hit him on the back of the head and everything went very dark.

"Sean, I'm picking something up on the police band," Trey called over the intercom as they slowly circled their downtown building. Everyone inside had been evacuated, and there were security teams all over the area looking for anything suspicious.

"They find the truck?"

"No, there's a jumper on the roof of the Grand Sierra."

"People jump from there all the time, why is this one special?"

"Because he's all tied up and there's another man with him."

"What?!"

"Security picked it up. They saw a guy being dragged up the stairwell to the roof level on their cameras. They called it in."

"Okay, so still not our problem."

"They traced the guy back to the room he rented. I recognized the last time. It's Betty's father."

"What?!" Sean said, turning to look at Trey. "Get us over there! Now!"

"I'll see what I can do, but the SWAT team is on their way, and the police have a helicopter already circling the building."

"Maybe we can take the guy out before he pushes Betty's dad over the side."

Peg laughed. "I'm not so sure you'd be doing her any favors, Sean!"

"I guess I didn't make myself clear," Trey said as they made the short dash over to the Grand Sierra. "Her dad isn't the guy tied up. They don't know who that is. Her father is the man that looks like he's about to throw him off the roof."

"Hand me that camera please?" Roxy said from the front right seat, pointing back to where her pack was.

Sean nodded and passed her the one they'd been planning to use to take pictures of any vehicles that looked suspicious so they could text them to the teams on the ground.

"I'm getting some grief from the P.D.," Trey said.

"Yeah, well, tell them to talk to our lawyer," Roxy growled. "As long as we're not in their way, they can't say anything. Tell 'em we're press."

"I think they recognize the big ass lion's head on the nose, Rox!" Trey laughed.

"Okay, I got them in my sights, hold steady a moment." Sean heard the camera take a series of shots. "Okay, give it a little more space and let's see what we got."

"Send it to Betty, she'll know who it is," Sean said.

"What? Are you insane? The poor girl has been through enough! I'll send it to my dad."

Pastor Cross groaned as he opened his eyes. The back of his head hurt something fierce! He tried to touch it, but found he couldn't move his hands, as his eyes suddenly focused and he noticed they were outside. On a roof. It was still nighttime, but it was bright enough that he could see…all the way down to the ground. *All* the way down to the ground.

"What's going on here!" He tried to say it with conviction, but it came out as more of a desperate plea.

"I had a few questions for you, Cross," Geoffrey growled in his ear.

"That's Pastor Cross! Have you lost your mind, Geoffrey?"

"Probably," Geoffrey said with a laugh. "Do you know what my daughter told me? Back when I disowned her?"

Pastor Cross shook his head, then winced. It hurt a lot. Geoffrey had been very quiet on that whole affair, other than saying his daughter had gone crazy.

"She said you got her pregnant."

"I did no such thing!"

"She said she lost the baby."

"That has nothing to do with me!"

"Because you shot her."

"Lies! It's all lies! Satan, the Deceiver, the Father of Lies, is behind all of this! I am a servant of our Lord! Nothing more! I'm a humble, righteous man!"

"I ran into Roy. Did you hear his wife is pregnant?"

Pastor Cross shook his head, what the hell was he ranting about now?

"Roy's sterile, Cross. I've known that all my life. We grew up together. Some disease he got as a teenager. But you didn't know that, did you?"

Pastor Cross felt the blood drain from his face.

"Yup, he didn't mind you gettin' one on his wife, 'cause they wanted a child and they thought you'd make a good 'biological' father. Just how many of the members' wives *were* you banging?"

"I did no such thing! I was simply teaching those women the error of their ways and the righteous path to our Lord!"

"More like the righteous path to your bed!" Geoffrey snarled. "You took advantage of them, used your power over all of us, to have your way with them."

"Do you know how much I've given up for all of you?" Pastor Cross yelled, trying to turn around and face Geoffrey. "I've spent hours upon hours tending to your souls! All of you! None of you were anything when I found you! You were just a broken down drunk! Your daughter was hanging around with the kind of men who would have used her and then just tossed her aside! Those other men, if they'd been paying their wives the attention they deserved, would never have ended up in my bed!

"It was my right as your shepherd! It was my right to take in those ewes who needed a strong man in their life! To take them and bed them and spread my seed amongst the faithful! I was doing them a favor! A service! For I am of the Lord, a holy and anointed one!"

"You know, I could have forgiven you all of this if you hadn't tried to kill them."

"They were in danger of falling into the hands of the devil! I had no choice! We all must make sacrifices, and that was mine!"

"Somehow I don't think God is going to see it like that."

"The Lord has forgiven me! He has told me so himself!"

"Oh, you talked to God then, did you?"

"Many times, the Lord has confided in me a great many things!"

"Then maybe we should go talk to him, you and I?" Geoffrey said in a suddenly soft voice.

"Yes! Let me go, we will go down to our church and pray, and I will reveal the wisdom and the words of the Lord to you in private!"

"Actually," Geoffrey said, leaning into Pastor Cross's back, "I was thinking more along the lines of the both of us going to meet him. Say right about…" Pastor Cross felt Geoffrey's hands wrap around him.

"NO!"

"…now," Geoffrey said and jumped off the side of the building, holding on tight to Cross. There was no way he was going to let that bastard get away from *this*.

Pastor Cross's eyes widened as the ground rushed up faster and faster to meet them.

"Holy shit! He jumped!" Sean swore, watching as the two men fell all the way down to the ground. The Grand Sierra's roof was about forty floors above the ground. It was a long drop.

"I've got Roxy's dad on the radio," Trey said.

Sean reached over and switched his headset to the radio. "What's up?"

"Two things. First, that guy with Betty's father? It's Pastor Cross, the guy who's leading them."

"Was leading them," Sean said.

"Oh, well. No great loss. Second, the police found an address written on a pad in the room Betty's father had been renting. The words 'Truck Bomb' were written under it."

"Oh, great. Where is it?"

"Off of Joule St., behind the airport. I'll text it to you so you can find it on your phone."

"I take it the police are on their way?"

"The police are waiting for the bomb squad."

"Okay, I'll get on it right away!" Sean said and, pulling out his phone, he looked at the address Bill had just sent him. Turning back to the intercom, he relayed the message.

"Where are we heading?" Trey asked.

"Joule Street, just west of Edison Way, and before South Rock. Look for a bunch of trucks with people milling about them."

"Okay, what's in them?"

"Ever hear of ANFO?"

"Damn…" Trey paused a moment. "Better cast some silence spells on us. If they hear us, it ain't gonna be safe unless we're way the hell up high."

"Well, I guess this means we found the missing fertilizer," Sean said and cast a silence spell on the helicopter.

"Let's get the doors open," Peg said. "Once we've found our target, hopefully a mass sleep spell will be all it takes to render everyone down there unconscious."

"Check your seatbelts, everyone," Sean warned, unlocking the side doors and sliding them back as he shifted into his hybrid form to help with night vision.

"I think I see something," Roxy said and pointed.

Sean looked over to the area and saw two trucks with a couple of people working on them. One was a straight truck, but the other was a large tanker truck.

"How the hell did they think they were going to get that up the hill?" Jolene said, peering over Peg.

"Look what's written on the side," Roxy said, shaking her head.

"I can't, I don't have night vision."

"It says 'Aviation Gas'," Roxy growled. "We have trucks like that coming up every day to fill up the helicopters!"

Shaking his head, Sean prepared the sleep spell. "We got lucky tonight, very lucky. We're going to need to up our security."

"Again," Roxy sighed.

"Yup," Sean said and cast the spell, then leaned back, panting a little. From all the way up here, it wasn't an easy spell.

"Call the police on the radio, Trey," Roxy said. "Tell them we slept everyone, and they need to get in here quick. That's one very massive bomb they've got sitting down there."

"On it!"

"Now what do you say we all go home?"

"I like that idea." Sean sighed. "Think maybe you could finally show me where my new office is?"

"What, can't find it on your own?" Roxy teased.

"Well, if you don't want to help me christen it, I could always ask Jo over there for help…"

"Oh! Well in that case, I'll be more than happy to!"

"Hey, don't forget about me!" Peg laughed.

"Me either," Jolene added.

Strange Bedfellows

Karl sighed and looked at the stream of people coming down the road. There were a pair of wolves sitting to either side of the road, and ten paces back from them there were two men with automatic rifles. All four were werewolves, and they were looking for demons hiding in the crowd, those poor souls who had been possessed, or worse yet, those traitors to the human race who were now willingly in league with the demons.

The last group was the hardest to spot, because they didn't give off any telltale scent. Supposedly the local mages were working on magical devices to detect them, but Karl wasn't exactly privy to that conversation. The dead bodies along the side of the road made it clear that they'd been finding people in at least the second category. He didn't see any spots of tar that showed where a demon had died.

"See anything?" Otto asked

"If I turn around, I see the road to Italy," Karl grumbled. "Which I should be on. Why am I doing this again?"

"Because you've got a guilty conscience that won't let you run away, and Raban has been using it to make you stay?"

"Is that why you're here?" Karl grumbled.

"Oh, no. I'm here because he ordered me to stay, and you don't argue with lions."

"Why not?"

"It's not allowed—as in, he told me I couldn't, so I can't."

"Just like that?"

Otto nodded. "Just like that. They made us, so when they want to, they can control us. Since Raban was ordered to hold Munich, he's been, well, how's that expression about fecal matter and hills go again?"

Karl nodded, he knew the one.

"So, tell me again. Who orders Raban around? Who gets to tell lions what to do?"

"The head lion, who else?"

"Where's he at?"

Otto shrugged. "No idea. Hell, until I met Raban, I'd never seen one in my entire life. I'd only heard the stories."

Karl shook his head and sighed. "I'd say you're all full of it, but I've seen too much not to believe you're telling me the truth. So why are we here again?"

"We're waiting for members of the Kitesh Korps."

"What a name for a gang," Karl said with snort. "They must be quite the characters if I've never seen anything about them in all my years of law enforcement."

"They're a magical gang, so I'd be surprised if you had."

"And what's magical about them?"

"Well, first off, Kitesh is an invisible city someplace on the border of Russia, I believe."

Karl raised an eyebrow and looked over at Otto. "Seriously?"

Otto nodded. "Yup. Some great magician, or group of them, cast a spell on the city a long, long time ago. I think they were hiding from the Mongols or something like that. Unfortunately rumor is, if you weren't a magician, you disappeared as well, so they lost a goodly part of their mundane population. That forced them to start preying on the neighboring cities and towns for their survival, and, well," Otto shrugged, "they never gave up that lifestyle."

"So they're all magic users?"

"Magic users, lycans, mythical beasts, fey, elves, goblins, what have you. Most magical gangs tend to be a mix-up of people who were either born into in, roped into it, sold into it, or joined willingly because they liked the lifestyle."

"Sounds like the kind of people we'd normally want to do without."

"But?" a voice called out.

"I don't see anything normal, and haven't in far too many days. Now show yourself so we can stop sitting on the side of the road."

"It's a strange day when I start taking orders from a constable," the voice said, and suddenly there was a slender and short, but incredibly handsome, older man with green-tinted skin.

"And a stranger one when he lets you ride in his car without arresting you," Otto replied. "I'm Otto; I'm a werewolf. That's Karl; he's a police officer and quite human.

"I'm Bilkie, call me Bilk for short."

"You're already short," Otto said with a grin.

"Yeah, 'cause people been calling me that all my life and I grew into it!" Bilkie said with a laugh.

"Let's get in the car," Karl said with a shake of his head. "If it's not impolite to ask, what are you anyways? I get the feeling you aren't human."

"Nope, I'm half goblin, half forest elf."

"You favor your mother's looks," Otto said.

"How'd ya' guess?"

"You're half elvish and you had to ask?"

Bilkie laughed again. "Clever punter, aren't ya? So where are we off to?"

"To see the lion in charge of Munich," Karl told him as he started up the car.

"Ah! I see the rumors are true; they've decided to put a hand in, haven't they? So what's your story, officer?"

"So many years of government service that I no longer have the brains to quit."

"So," Otto said, turning in the front seat to talk to Bilkie in the back, "how bad is Berlin?"

"In all me days and nights, for as long as I shall live, I will never ever forget what I saw there," Bilkie said in a voice that made shivers run up and down Karl's spine. "The city is gone, completely gone. The buildings may remain, but the people? They're all cattle now, them's that're still alive, that is. We lost half our crew gettin' out of there. Me friend Horace, he was a wolf just like you, he died saving the lot of us that got away from there."

"So they've taken over the government?" Karl asked, though he knew the answer.

"Oh, yeah, they've either taken them or eaten them. Honestly, though? Looking back? I think they got a lot of those government types years ago. Years ago."

Karl just shook his head and drove them back to the mayor's office Raban had co-opted.

Karl followed Otto and Bilkie up to Raban's office after he'd parked the car. He found he was doing a lot of that nowadays.

"Ah! So you're from the Kitesh Korps!" Raban said, coming around the desk and shaking hands with Bilkie. The size difference between the two, as Raban openly went around in his hybrid form at all times now, was rather shocking.

"You must be Raban. Bilkie's the name. So what brings you to summon'in our help?"

"If there's anybody who knows what's been going on in the magical as well as mundane underside of the cities around here, it'd be you. We need to know what we're up against, and what little secrets are out there that we can put to our best use."

"Ya' must know that there are Lithos in this city already?"

Raban snorted. "We're still more than a bit pissed at the Lithos; they should have known better than to go after one of our own."

"Well, I hate to be the one to stand in their defense, but I don't think they rightly knew it be a lion there were chasing. And, begging your pardon, but considering how many of them said lion killed, I'd think they'd be lookin' for any chance to make amends. Before ye' kill the rest o' them."

Raban snorted. "I had no idea you two even talked to each other."

Bilkie gave them a weak smile and shrugged. "We do some business, it's just the nature of our particular occupations."

"Well then, you can tell them if they apologize, all will be forgiven, though I would caution them to steer *very* clear of Valens. Guy has a bit of a temper."

"Oi, not like any other lion does, am I right?"

"Oh, some of us are downright reasonable, though of late he rarely is." Raban laughed then. "Our leader stuck him in something of a position, and he doesn't waste any opportunity to give him grief over it. In fact, he's why I'm here."

"Does that mean you don't want to be here?" Karl asked.

"No. He made a good argument, only reason why he won it. I'm just glad I wasn't the one who made it. Now, how many did you bring with you, and where are they?"

"Twenty-three of us from Berlin, and another couple dozen we picked up on the road here. They'll all be on the way to a place we keep here for when we trade with the Lithos."

Raban nodded. "Tonight I'd like to gather those of you with the most knowledge on the area as well as find out what you saw. We don't just need help with our northern borders, we need help with rooting out anything or anyone those djevels have touched or corrupted."

"And who knows the corrupted better than the corrupt, right?" Bilkie said with a chuckle.

"The magic users are producing items that will help track them down, but you know they're not the type to go to the places where they need to, to find these things."

"Oi, you got that right. Well, I'll take my leave then and find me mates, and we'll be back about an hour after nightfall."

Raban nodded and smiled. "Thank you."

Otto and Karl watched him leave.

"You know he's going to want something from you after this is over," Karl said, looking back at Raban.

"Of course he will, and we'll make sure to give them something fitting."

"There'is another thing that's occurred to me as well."

"Oh?"

"How much longer do you think we'll have gas for our cars? Or even electricity for the lights?

Things are going to start falling apart any day now with no one to maintain things."

Raban sighed and nodded. "Guess I better call in the city engineers and see what they can figure out. Otto, find the horse clan head and tell them we need him to gather all the normal horses in town for when the fuel runs out."

Otto nodded and left the room.

"As for you," Raban said, turning to Karl, "as long as the phones and radios continue to work, check in with the officers still alive to the north. Find out what they know, warn them when you can, and invite them here if you think they'll come."

"You want to bring them here?"

Raban nodded. "We're going to need a lot more police officers here to keep the peace with the number of refugees that have been pouring in. If I put any of my soldiers on it," Raban grimaced, "the results won't be at all pretty."

"I'll see what I can do," Karl said.

Ξ

King Sladd sat in his throne room as his six princes entered. Each of them moved quickly to their customary position in the room, then prostrated themselves before him. Usually he would have waited for them to be here first, but what he had to tell them was important. So by avoiding that little display of power, they would get the message and be in a more receptive mode.

Lately his spies had been telling him things about Prince Talt that had him growing concerned. During this last storsindet gateway, Prince Talt had committed even less of his forces than the others had, and none of his most experienced leaders.

King Sladd waited until they'd all found their places, their advisors forming up and prostrating behind them. Once they'd settled into position, their eyes on the floor, King Sladd made a short motion with his hand.

"You!" one of the guards called out, "Eyes down!" and he stepped forward and hit one of Prince Talt's advisors in the back of the head, driving him down.

"I meant nothing by it!" said Svatick, the advisor, surprising King Sladd with his response; he had obviously realized a denial would be useless here.

"Then you admit to your impertinence!" King Sladd roared. "Bring him here before me!"

Another guard stepped over, and the two of them grabbed Svatick by the shoulders and literally dragged him forward, not giving him a chance to get to his feet. King Sladd had his own spies in Prince Talt's forces, and two of them had shared their suspicions that Svatick was the advisor who was pushing Prince Talt to consider revolt.

"The law is clear!" King Sladd said, standing as the guards threw Svatick to the ground before him.

"I meant no insult, Your Majesty! Your commanding presence…"

Svatick's voice stopped instantly as King Sladd's iron-edged sword came down and split his skull. King Sladd looked around the room as he all but inhaled Svatick's essence, dealing him a true death.

Everyone else's eyes were riveted to the floor. He doubted he had fooled any of them, but perhaps Prince Talt would take heed and realize there were limits upon him.

"Arise!" he called and sat down as they stood.

"I have called you here today to inform you my wizards of the helliges have forecast that this most recent storsindet was the last one we'll see. That means from this point forward, we shall utilize the lille helliges."

"Why, Your Majesty?" Prince Lykta asked. "You have counseled us until now to avoid wasting resources on them."

"Because now we may gain from them, where before we did not," King Sladd said, looking over the room. "The amount of damage we could do before was nothing; it would not make a difference, because all we had to deal with was more of the lille gates. But the master gateway will open soon. The lions have arrayed their strength all around it. If we can weaken them enough now, they will not be able to respond in full strength when we deploy through the master gate."

"What will our order of deployment be, Your Majesty?" Prince Skarm asked.

"Princes Talt, Skarm, Spis, and Lagereld, you four will line up your forces to go through the gateway and fight until they have either succeeded or been removed. The rest of you shall sally forth through the lille helliges as they should appear, to harass and weaken the enemy. I do not think they will be able to deal with the two gates being open for long, so they will have to abandon either guarding the master gateway, or the lilles. My thoughts lead me to believe that those using the lille will see our first success."

"And what of your soldiers, King Sladd?" Prince Lagereld asked.

"My troops will be behind yours. I am sure by the time you are finished with them, Prince

Lagereld, the resistance of the lions will be no more.

"Does this mean you plan to personally take the field?" Prince Spis inquired.

"Eventually, yes, I believe I will. It has been a long, long time since a permanent gateway has been bound to one of the sacred hunting grounds. I will be giving this my personal attention to make sure we do not fail.

"Also consider this: The more of *our* troops are in the hunting grounds when the permanent gateway forms, the *easier* it will be for me to hold *both* sides of it. Which will profit all of us. Understood?"

"Yes, Your Majesty!" all six princes said, prostrating themselves before him.

King Sladd smiled. "Now, be about my work!" he said, dismissing them. He was curious as to what his spies would be reporting to him as all six discussed the execution that had taken place today.

Entangled

Sean sat at his desk looking at the reports. A week from now, the *real* fight would start: the main gateway would open somewhere out there. In these last few months, it was getting to be more than he could deal with. He'd thought he'd made his life easier back when he'd pushed all the business paperwork off onto Deidre, but running a war was a lot more work than he could have ever predicted. Even with all the logistics decisions being funneled through the staff General Baker had left him.

Even with Chad, Maitland, and now Jack, Bill, Roloff, and Claudia helping him by taking the lead on most of the strategic and tactical planning.

Because he was the one at the top, the one in charge. He was the final authority. The one who had to approve everything. *Everyone* deferred to him, even the regular military officers now. At times he hated it, hated that at the ripe old age of twenty-two, he was the ultimate authority. That he was always expected to have the answer when no one else knew what to do. The one who had to get up in front of everyone, damn near all the time now, and show them they could in fact do their jobs without him around to hold their hands.

About the only people who didn't defer to him were the mid-level bureaucrats who worked for the city. The mayor at least did what she could to help with that; she wasn't an idiot, she saw the money and the power that he controlled, and knew staying on his good side would mean something when the next election came around. Sean also got the impression she cared more about the people she represented than those who'd been appointed to their jobs or risen to their level of incompetence, but who now couldn't be fired because they were civil servants and it took an act of god to get one of them fired.

He also missed being able to just ask the First for a solution whenever he wasn't sure what to do. He'd had to make so many snap decisions in the last month, he knew he had to have gotten some of them wrong, but apparently the saying was true: Better a bad decision now than no decision at all.

But like it or not, he was the one who'd gotten them this far, and he sure as *hell* knew better than to give it all over to someone else. He was the one they knew, the one they trusted, the one who had gotten them all to this point. He couldn't walk away; he owned it, all of it, whether he wanted it or not.

"Time for the staff meeting, Sean," Peg said, sticking her head into his office. Somehow she'd decided, or they'd decided—they didn't consult with him when they made those kinds of decisions—they'd decided she was going to be the one playing roadblock, or secretary. Sometime about when they'd decided he couldn't use his workshop as an office anymore, and he couldn't go back to sharing with Deidre.

"I'm coming." He sighed, grabbing his now ever-present notebook as he got up and headed for the door.

"Did we keep you up too late last night?" Peg teased as he stopped to give her a kiss before continuing on.

"It's not that," Sean said with a shake of his head. "It's just," he shook his head again, "look at me. I'm buried in paperwork, plans, requests, all this stuff I need to approve. Everyone wants my guidance, my approval. I'm twenty-two, Peg. I spent most of my life struggling to barely get by, and now I'm the one with all the answers."

"You're the victim of your own success," Peg said with a grin and hugged him back. "You may be young, but you're not stupid, and so far you've managed to handle everything that's been thrown at you. People like a proven winner, and right now, you're the only one they've got."

"Yeah, but what happens when I lose?" Sean said, looking at her a little worried.

"Same thing that happened all the other times you lost," she said and gave him a smack on the butt. "You'll try again. Now stop frowning, it'll make people wonder what's wrong."

"I'll just tell them you wouldn't give me a quickie before the meeting," Sean said with a smirk.

"Oh, like they'd believe *that*!" Peg laughed.

Shaking his head, Sean put an arm around her and headed off to the conference room. At least he was smiling now.

"We really need to have someone sit in your office with you; you start to brood too much when you're alone these days," Peg said, looking thoughtful. "I'll talk to Rox and Dae about it."

"Un-huh." Sean nodded to the guard standing by the door to the conference room. Cali and Estrella had decided that the days of lax security were over a month ago when someone had killed a bonde found sneaking around by itself a couple miles away.

"Morning, everyone," Sean said as he walked around the table. Coming to the head of it, he sat down. "So, what's the analysis on both yesterday's and last Sunday's gates?"

"They're trying to wear us down for a big push when the main gate opens," Jack said.

Chad nodded in agreement. "It's like dropping an artillery barrage on the opposing side just before you attack."

"Isn't that kind of tipping their hand?" Sean asked. Up until last Sunday's gate, all the small gates had been pretty much left unused by the djevels. Only the large gates had been seeing action.

"We already know they're coming, Nephew," Maitland pointed out.

Sean looked around the table. "Suggestions?"

"I don't think we're going to see any more large gates," Deidre said.

"Oh?"

"I've been running a statistical analysis on the gates, and with only two left before we enter the main gate cycle, the odds are heavily against it."

"Also," Chad picked up, "if the enemy thought there was another large gate in the mix this close to the next cycle, they'd be saving their strength for that instead."

"So we have a gate cycle starting Friday, followed by another on the first, which is Monday," Sean said, looking over at the chart on the east wall with the big gateway sequence calendar.

"What are we going to do about them? If they're planning a big push come the fourth, the last thing we want is to still be licking our wounds when they show up."

"Tac-nukes?" Jack suggested.

Chad immediately shook his head. "I'd like to hold off on letting them in on that particular surprise until the main gate opens."

"They already know about them," Jack said with a shrug. "They've been here for years; I don't think there's any weapon in the inventory they don't know about."

Sean smiled. "He's got you there, you know."

"They may know about them, but I doubt they think we're going to be willing to use them on our own soil. Not yet at least. Besides, how are we going to get one? Do you think the president is just going to hand you one?"

"Good point." Jack sighed.

"That reminds me," Sean said with a sigh, pulling out a pencil and making a note in his notebook.

"About what?" Roxy asked looking over his shoulder.

"I need to ask the president for a bunch of nukes."

"Seriously?"

"Sooner or later we're going to need them. If I don't ask now, when we do need them it'll take far too long to get one."

"What about the 'divine wrath of the lions'?" Claudia asked.

"That's a lot trickier to deal with than you realize," Sean said with a heavy sigh.

"Also, it's something they *don't* know about," Roxy pointed out to everyone there. "So it's best if we save it for when we *really* need it."

"But you already hit them with it once, didn't you?"

"They don't know that," Estrella piped up. "They think it was some sort of magical attack."

"Why don't you just continue to use artillery on them?" Bill asked.

Maitland shook his head. "Eventually they're going figure out they can use shield spells to deflect them, so until we've handled that…"

"Plus," Chad added, "I'd like to hold off on the arty until the main gate. That stuff isn't unlimited, so I'd rather they spent the next week prepping for the big fight."

"What about all them tanks ya' got sitting out to the south of the city?" Daelyn asked.

"We don't know how well they'll do," Chad replied. "We're still working out how to best employ them."

"Well, maybe it's time we started learnin?"

"Daelyn has a point," Roloff said, getting Sean's interest. Roloff didn't tend to get too involved in these meetings, as the dwarves hadn't taken too big of a role in the fighting yet. Mostly they'd send a unit or two out to get experience. In the general scheme of things, the dwarves weren't as mobile as lycans were, so they were being set up to play defense. Once they had a fixed battle space, that is. Right now Reno was surrounded by a hell of a lot of very well dug in dwarves.

Chad pondered that, then looked up at Sean.

"What are you looking at me for?" Sean asked with a sigh.

"If we roll the tanks out there, they're going to take a pasting, I'm sure."

"Yeah, but we haven't been using them, so if there's anything we can afford to lose right now, it's those tanks, and you know it."

"Yeah, I know it," Chad sighed, "I just hate being the one to have to make those decisions."

Sean nodded. "Yeah, it's tough at the top. Welcome to the big leagues, right?"

Chad shook his head while giving Sean a lopsided grin. "You got that right. Okay, we'll move all the tanks up, along with all the Strykers and the Abrams we have. Roloff, I want you to take command of their deployments and work with their commanders on tactics."

"You want me?" Roloff said, looking surprised.

"Yeah, I need a sneaky bastard with an understanding of armor, and you've already got your guys dug in. I was hoping you'd appreciate the challenge."

Roloff nodded and smiled. "Iffen that's what you want, I think I can find the time."

"Great," Sean said. "I'll leave that to the rest of you to figure out. Next point of business: the main gate. It should open sometime after midnight on the fourth."

"It doesn't follow the random cycle of the previous gates?" Claudia asked.

Sean shook his head. "No, it will open within hours of midnight. It'll start out as a small gate, then over the next ninety days it'll grow to full size."

"We still get the small gates, correct?" Maitland asked, looking at his notes.

"Yes, every three days, but every nine cycles we get a period with no gates."

"That's twenty-seven days?"

"Yup. Then after nine months, we enter a six-month period where the small gates become medium gates. After about eight of those, the permanent gate opens."

"That's the one we have to worry about," Estrella said.

"Yeah. That's the one we have to worry about. We're not exactly clear on how it works, but if it stays open more than forty-eight hours, we're fairly certain the main gateway collapses and this new one becomes permanent."

"What aren't you clear on?" Claudia asked.

"Well, we believe both it and the main gateway will stay open for twenty-four hours, no matter what the djevels have accomplished. *But*," Sean sighed and shook his head, looking over at her, "we don't know if the main gateway will collapse before the second twenty-four hours are up if the conditions for permanence are met."

Estrella spoke up, "You have to understand, the permanent gateway has never become permanent before. Well, not here at least. There are gateways out there between other realms that are permanent, but we're not exactly sure how they happened. So no one really knows exactly when during that forty-eight-hour period the 'conditions' for the gateway to become permanent must be met…"

"…or if there's any warning we'll get beforehand so we'll know we're in trouble and need to take action before the test for those conditions takes place," Sean finished.

"Well, that doesn't sound good." Claudia sighed.

"No, but it's what we're up against."

They spent the next hour going over preparations for the main gateway opening. Deidre had been running a statistical analysis of the gateway locations and, using information some of the lions had passed on, had projected a likely area for the gateway to open. If that worked out, it would definitely put them in a far better position than they normally were when a gateway opened.

"Next topic," Sean said once they got that one finished, "is Germany."

Everyone around the table flinched.

"I guess I'll start off," Estrella said. "Munich is still holding on. The mages guild there has managed to put up a strong enough ward that it has encouraged the djevels to look elsewhere—for now. My brother Raban is there now, and he's got almost a thousand lycans with him, the mayor has given full amnesty to any and all lycans, not that I think anyone would enforce that law.

"All of the United States Army units from Stuttgart have fallen back towards Heidelberg. They're trying to form a line down to the French border, and points further south. The lycans who fled to France and Switzerland have moved up to their borders. There's been a great deal of support from the magical community there, as well as the elves and the dwarves.

"To the north of Heidelberg, they've formed a defensive line back towards Bonn and Cologne. Refugees are still fleeing west in great numbers. Belgium and the Netherlands are trying to shore up their borders with what they have along the west. Oland, Prague, and Austria are attempting to do the same to the east."

"Maitland?" Sean asked.

"Well, the northern Faerie in Denmark and the other Nordic countries have been moving south into northern Germany. They haven't encountered any djevels yet. Those in the UK and Eastern Europe have finally agreed to join the fight, so that's northern France, Belgium, and the Netherlands. Those who live to the west of Poland in those northern states are coming, but it will be weeks before they'll be able to join the fight."

"Jack, what have your contacts in the Pentagon told you?"

"Well, first off, they're *finally* going to send us an intelligence officer, who will have direct access to the data we've been asking for. But the general gist of it seems to be that they have packs of demons,"

"Djevels," Cali corrected.

"Whatever. They have packs of them roaming an area from Munich all the way up to Hanover. They haven't come too far west yet, but no one is sure how long the major western cities up around Dortmund can be protected. Berlin, however, is a complete write-off. The army units there were able to fight their way out and are on their way to Hamburg. Once they got past the city limits, the enemy stopped following them. Oddly enough, Dresden and Leipzig have been totally ignored."

"Do they have any kind of estimate on the number of djevels there?" Sean asked.

"Well, they're pretty sure there's thousands of them in Berlin. Possibly as many as ten thousand. The rest of the country? It's probably only a thousand at most. It's just the lack of anyone able to stand up to them has given them free reign over the countryside."

Estrella picked it back up. "There've been twenty-seven small roaming gates that opened in random areas of Germany as of last Tuesday. It wasn't until the middle of April that anyone even knew we had a problem there. If the djevels were able to put, say, two hundred through each gate, that would give them at least five thousand in the country."

"Why do you think there's so many of them in Berlin?" Claudia asked.

"We're pretty sure a fair deal of the government was compromised," Estrella said with a sigh. "They had a lot of control and power over the city, and that's a lot of free food just waiting to be claimed. The First and the others think the djevels will use the power they gain from consuming the population to build a stronghold there and eventually breed more."

"Which would indicate that the ones roaming the countryside are there more to create a barrier between Berlin and the military forces that could attack them," Chad suggested.

"If that's the case, there would have to be some high-ranking djevels in Berlin now," Cali said.

"Obviously," Estrella agreed. "I've discussed this with the First and the others. They've been thinking along the same lines."

"How's the fight going down in South America?" Bill asked.

"They've got it well under control," Sean said. "I spoke to the lion in charge last night. Things are still playing out as they're used to down there. They don't expect much of a push until the main gateway opens, and the elves have been showing up in force the last month. They've turned out a large portion of their fighters for this."

"So what do we do about Germany?" Oak asked.

"Nothing," Sean said with a shake of his head. "Our job is right here in front of us. In a few more days, I suspect we're going to be way too busy to worry about anything else."

Everyone nodded, agreeing quietly.

"Well, I think that's it for today," Sean said, standing up. "Meeting adjourned."

"Now what?" Estrella asked as Sean checked his notes.

"Now I get to fly into Reno and meet with the mayor, the chief of police, and all the rest of them," Sean grumbled. He really was beginning to hate these bi-weekly meetings with the mayor and the city's different department heads. Getting them to do anything was like pulling teeth.

"Bill, you coming with me, or Claudia?"

"I want to discuss a few things with her," Bill said. "I'll ride in with her."

Sean nodded. "Cali, Dae, once Travis' team calls it clear, we'll be heading out."

"Can I come along?" Estrella asked.

Sean smiled. "Of course you can, Stell. I need to check on some things; I'll meet you on the helipad in a few."

Heading back to his office, Sean strapped on his pistol, checked to make sure he had a couple of wands, checked his email and other messages, put on a nice jacket to help conceal the gun, then dropped his notebook on the desk. Last thing he wanted was to forget that at the mayor's office; they'd probably have a field day with the information inside, he'd written way too many nasty comments about some of the people there in it.

"You ready, Peg?" Sean asked. He always brought her along so no one would be able to make any recordings or eavesdrop on the meeting.

"Yup! Travis just called, let's go!"

Sean gave a nod and led the way out to the helipad, where one of the Black Hawks was warming up.

"You don't look happy, My Husband," Cali observed as they drew near.

"I hate having to play politics," Sean said with a sigh. That was what this meeting was about really, politics. He needed to stay on the good side of the mayor and the rest of the civil servant bosses to ensure things got done.

Which had been getting harder and harder for the last couple of weeks, now that things were starting to draw to a head.

"Then don't," Cali said with a smile.

"Easier said than done," he said with a shake of his head. Thankfully they were close enough to the loud helicopter now to make conversation difficult. Sean helped Peg in first, then Cali, following her in. Daelyn and Estrella were already on board. Sitting down, he put on a headset and buckled his seatbelt as one of the crew closed the door.

"I see she finally got you to give up your seat, Trey," Peg said over the intercom.

Looking up, Sean noticed that Daelyn was in the pilot's seat; Trey was now in the copilot's.

"She's gotta learn sooner or later!" Trey laughed.

"But we're all in here, too! *And* we're landing on a rooftop!" Estrella grumbled. Sean knew she still wasn't one hundred percent comfortable in helicopters.

"If I don't give her the tough ones, she won't learn, now will she?" Trey replied with another laugh.

Sean could see that Daelyn was totally focused on what she was doing; he'd only seen that look on her face when she was driving her 'Cuda at the limits, or trying to brain him one with Maxwell.

"Let's go, Dae," Sean told her over the intercom, leaning back in his seat and getting out his phone to check messages.

"You seem pretty calm," Estrella said, still looking nervous as Cali smirked.

"It's just a helicopter ride, Stell. She goes faster than this thing in her car when she and Rox go out for pizza. Right, Dae?"

"Oh, just you wait!" Daelyn said as she lifted off. Sean was rather impressed; she was almost as smooth as Trey, and she'd only been at this a couple of weeks. "Once I got this thing figured out, I'm gonna go so fast it'll make yer eyes bleed!"

"And here you thought your Summit Racing bill was bad!" Peg said, laughing.

"I'd ask whose idea it was to get her an even *more* expensive hobby, but I don't think I want to know," Sean said, not noticing Cali's sudden grin.

It didn't take them long to get to city hall, where the mayor's office was. They didn't actually land on the roof; Sean wasn't sure it could handle the weight of a Black Hawk. They did land in the City Plaza next door, which had recently been repainted with two helipads. There were a fair number of guards there nowadays; ostensibly Colonel Tibbets had put them there to keep anyone from getting hurt by one of the helicopters, but the real reason was to secure an area with a lot of important people coming through.

"You coming in with us Dae?" Sean asked.

"Nah, Trey's gonna have me do a few practice landings around town."

"Have fun," Sean said and patted her on the shoulder as one of Travis' team ran up and opened the door.

Getting out, Sean and the girls noticed the amount of armed troops downtown had grown once again, and a *lot* of them were in their hybrid forms. That only made sense, as the fey armor was fit solely to that form, as it was the one they'd be fighting in.

"Who thought we'd be seeing stuff like this a year ago?" Peg asked, looking around. "The very idea of lycans being out in the open would have given my dad a heart attack."

"I don't think he'd have been very keen on the idea of a demon invasion, either," Sean said with a chuckle.

"Is he the one…?" Estrella started.

"Our husband beat to death with his own arm," Cali finished.

"The whole ripping his arm off probably killed him first," Peg mused, "but still, it's the thought that counts!" she finished with a wink and a grin.

Shaking his head, Sean led the way into the building. The guard on duty nodded and buzzed them through the side door; Sean, Cali, and Estrella were carrying way too much hardware to go through the metal detector. Peg most likely had a few things as well, Sean mused.

The trip upstairs went without notice or much comment. Sean's face really wasn't that well known around here yet, he'd managed to keep a fairly low profile, in his human form at least. The mayor's secretary knew who he was, however, so he was waved right in without comment.

Claudia and Bill were already there, of course, as well as Mayor Schiere; Sid, the chief of police; Ben, the chief of the fire department; Debbie, the mayor's stenographer; her aide Jerry; a few other department heads Sean couldn't remember the names of; and most of the city council.

"Good morning, everyone," Sean said, nodding. Apparently the meeting had started without him, which was a little annoying, but he'd cope. Hopefully it meant he'd get out of here early for a change.

"Sorry I'm late. Now, where are we?"

"We were discussing some of the structures you want us to build," said one of the men, who

Sean recalled was the head of the city's civil engineering department.

"Ah, okay," Sean said with a nod.

"Well, we have a few problems," the man started, then he immediately launched into all the reasons they couldn't do what Sean had wanted them to do. All of which had actually been drawn up by some of Roloff's dwarves, who had a fairly comprehensive idea of what the city had, and what it could do.

Seeing as several of them worked for the city's engineering group as contractors.

Sean just sat there and listened while the man lectured him for almost an hour, copping quite the attitude, some of the others occasionally feeling a bit emboldened by it to join in a little here and there. It was everything Sean could do at first to not just punch the guy in the face. But he had to keep telling himself that they weren't lycans, they weren't his people. They didn't work for him.

By the time they were done, Sean had given up and really just didn't care anymore. He'd given them a nice list of things that needed to be done to help secure the city when the inevitable attack came, and these people, who could not possible ignore the sounds of the shelling and the bombing that happened twice a week, just didn't seem to get it.

It's like they had no sense of survival at all.

"Mayor Schiere, is there anything you can do about these manpower problems and other shortages that," Sean waved at the guy, "he's been going on about?"

"The union has been making a lot of noise." The mayor sighed. "They're threatening to strike if we push them any harder."

"Has it occurred to them," Sean turned back to the man at that point, "or you, whatever your name is, that these things are a matter of survival? That people are going to die?"

"You don't know that!" he countered.

"Actually, once martial law is declared, you'll simply be shot as a traitor," Sean said with an exasperated sigh, "so, yes, I think I do."

That got quite the response from everyone at the meeting, and it definitely *wasn't* the one Sean had been hoping for after listening to the man prattle on for over an hour.

"Sean! That was uncalled for!" the mayor said as the others also protested. Sean could see that both Bill and Claudia were looking less than pleased as well.

"No, what was uncalled for was making me sit through this man's hour-long excuse for why he won't do his job. If you don't want me to defend Reno, then I won't. But because this *is* my home—I grew up here, after all—I'd thought I'd make the attempt.

"Guess I should apologize for wasting your time."

"You don't have any say in what happens here!" the man said.

Shaking his head, Sean stood up, sighing. "And that's where you're wrong. Every single soldier outside in uniform answers to me.

"Not to the mayor, not to the governor, not even to the president. Good luck, all of you."

Turning, Sean walked out the door as Cali and Estrella quickly followed.

"Well, that was smart," Peg said, looking over the rest of the group. "I think all of you need to remember that 'young man' you're all so dismissive of has killed more people with his own two hands than most armies in the world today.

"I won't even get into the thousands of deaths he's had to order." Peg turned to look at the head of the civil engineering group who had been annoying Sean for the last hour.

"And if I were you, Justin, I'd be leaving town like, *right now*."

"What? You're saying he'll kill me?"

Peg laughed. "Sean? No. Apparently he's already decided you're not worth the trouble. But you have to remember one of his wives is a renowned assassin, and another is well known for slaughtering anybody who pisses her off. Almost all of the rest are fighters, and you better believe tonight we're all going to be racing to see who claims your head first.

"Pleasant dreams, asshole."

Turning on her heel, Peg walked out, a smile that was all teeth on her face.

"She…she wasn't kidding, was she?" Mayor Schiere asked, her face white.

"Damn, I better try and stop this," Bill swore, and getting up, he ran out the door after them.

"Really put your foot in it there, Justin," Claudia said, gathering up her notes and sweeping them into her briefcase. "Damn," she said with a shake of her head, "and we just got the casino opened, too."

"You don't think he's really going to abandon Reno, do you?" Mayor Schiere asked, gaping.

"Sounds to me like he just did. But honestly? I'm not so sure that's a bad idea. Better break out those evacuation plans, Your Honor. You're going to need them."

"Sean, you can't be serious!" Bill said, running up to Sean as they left the building. Sean had seen the smile on Peg's face when she caught up with them at the elevator, but figured whatever it was she'd said, they'd all probably deserved it. He had been starting to think that maybe he finally was in over his head, and this meeting had all but confirmed it.

Sean turned and looked at his father-in-law. "Right now, Dad, I don't want to talk about it."

"They're not lycans or magic users, Son! You can't expect them to understand!"

"They can hear the bombing and the shelling every night we're out there fighting, Dad. If they can't understand, maybe I'm just not the right person for the job."

"If the mayor can't keep her people on a leash, maybe *she's* not the right person for the job," Estrella grumbled.

"That man was very rude," Cali agreed, scowling.

"Still," Bill said.

Sean raised his hand, he could see their Black Hawk was coming in for a landing, Daelyn was still flying.

"Our ride's here, we can talk about it later," Sean said, making a beeline for the helicopter as Travis' security team took up their positions and escorted them.

Bill looked at Peg, who just smiled and winked at him. He knew Cali was an assassin, his daughter had told him, though she hadn't told him of anybody she'd killed. But Bill knew enough to know Cali wasn't an innocent. None of them were, not even his own little Roxy.

Would someone kill Justin tonight? If they did, it would definitely send a shockwave through the entire city government, maybe even the state government. Peg had all but said he was going to be killed by *somebody*. She'd laid it out there for all the world to see, with not a single concern for the fact that the room was full of witnesses, one of whom was the chief of police of the city in which the murder would be taking place.

But, and there was always a 'but', it might just wake the rest of them up and make them understand what was on the line here, and what the punishments were for putting the lives of others at risk because your sense of self-importance was so big that you had to get into a dick-waving contest with people who were in a whole other league.

#

Card watched those around him carefully as they moved down the street. Infiltrating the ALS hadn't been all that hard, really. He'd learned a lot working as a Prime for the Vestibulum, where he'd been expected to assassinate all sorts of troublemakers, ones who could wield magic and were as paranoid as they came. All that training had made this as easy as a walk in the park.

All he'd had to do was show up at the events and throw a few cokes at some of the 'dirty lycan scum'. When things got a little out of hand, mostly at the prodding of the others, he'd held back and helped the rank and file. His 'restraint' had been noticed, and he'd made friends with a couple of the girls, who were obviously attracted to him.

The guys in the group had then been forced to make friends with him in order to prevent their girlfriends from ending up with him instead of them.

The whole thing had been rather funny. To be honest, he enjoyed the work; it was a lot more in line with what he'd spent his life learning to do. That lion gal, Tisha, she only scared him a little, not like that Sean guy did. After that one time Sean had helped him out, Card had carefully avoided him. While the others told him Sean didn't blame him, he'd still heard enough stories that he didn't want to put it to the test.

But Steve? Card had met him once, face to face, when Steve had come out to Eruditio to meet with the team there and give them their orders. Card liked Steve, he was irreverent and sneaky as all shit, and as slippery as a used car salesman. All the things that made a good Prime. When this was over, he was going to see if he could be put on Steve's staff. Quick, Tank, and the others, they would have liked Steve.

He shook his head and went back to watching the others. They had a big target today; Steve was being interviewed at one of the local TV stations for one of their news shows. Someone there had 'spilled' the information, and they were going to protest outside the building during the show.

"I tell ya, these filthy animals think they can get away with anything!" Howard, one of the guys on the team, said to Card as they came in sight of the TV station's building.

"I know, right?" Card grumbled back to them. "I tell ya', we really need to stop pussyfooting around and teach those curs a lesson!"

"Down with the curs!" said Julie, who was actually another werewolf working with Card, and smiled at him.

"Yeah! Down with the curs!" Howard agreed, with a glance at Julie. Card knew Howard had the hots for her. He'd told Julie to flirt with Howard, just a little, to show a little interest and string him along.

"I really wish they'd let us do something more!" Howard continued. "Instead of just protesting! We need to be more like those folks at the National Mall last weekend!"

"You're right," Julie said, egging him on. "We need to take action! *Real* action!"

"You want action?" Card said. "I'll show you some action, then maybe you and me?"

Card almost laughed at the look Howard shot him while Julie smiled.

"I like a man of action," Julie said, dangling the hook. Now all Card had to do was make sure Howard took it, and after years of dealing with pack dynamics, Card was positive he could help that along.

They spread out as they got there; they all had signs to wave as they marched around in front of the building, chanting their slogans.

"That Julie is a little hottie, ain't she, Howard?" Card said, acting as if he had no idea at all about Howard's own lusts. "Man, I bet if I did something outrageous, I'd get in her pants tonight!"

Card watched as Howard considered that, a fleeting look of jealously passing over his face. Card gave Julie the high sign.

"I'm gonna get us some water, be right back!" Card said, and then moved away from Howard over to the cooler full of water bottles as Julie came by and chatted him up a little, after making sure the group's leaders where out of earshot.

"So, you like a man of action?" Card heard Howard ask Julie.

Julie gave him a look, then glanced over at Card, before looking back at Howard, letting him see her weighing the two of them.

"You gonna do something? Something *nasty*?" Julie asked in a soft voice that Card only heard because of his enhanced lycan hearing.

"Course I'm gonna do something!" Howard boasted. "You just watch!"

"Ooooo," Julie said, laying it on thick. "You do that, and maybe later tonight?"

Howard grinned and nodded.

Card almost laughed; it was way too easy. Now it was time to move in for the kill. He watched as Julie gave Howard a pat on the arm, and then sashayed off with her sign, shaking her butt for Howard's benefit. He waited a minute and came back over to Howard, handing him a bottle of water.

"We need to do something, something *nasty*," Howard said, giving Card a challenging look as he opened the bottle and took a drink of water.

Card nodded in agreement, a serious look on his face. "I hear you, brother. I got an idea, man, but it's pretty nasty."

"Oh? What?"

"You know lycans can't handle silver, right?"

"Seriously? I thought that was a myth?"

Card snorted. "It ain't. That's how those mages were keeping them as slaves until the president freed 'em all. They've been keeping it a secret, but I looked it up online last night. It's on the ALS website!"

"Really?"

"Yeah, check it out on your phone, Bro, shit kills 'em dead."

"So you got some on you?"

"Yeah, I got a couple of silver bullets."

"You got a gun?" Howard said, looking shocked.

Card snorted. "I got two derringers. Best I could find around here. Drove up to West Virginia last night. I figure between the two of them, I ought to hit the bastard once."

"Which bastard?"

"The one in charge, of course! He was there when they cut our brothers down in that attack on the highway!"

Howard nodded; everyone knew about the highway attack, though the ALS people had come to believe they were the innocents now in that fiasco.

"How are you going to get past his bodyguards?" Howard asked after a moment. They'd all seen Steve at events before, and they knew he always had two bodyguards with him.

"I was hoping if I charged in there real quick with my little guns blazing, I'd take him out before they stopped me."

"What if I helped?" Howard said.

"What?"

"Give me one of your guns. I'll take out the bodyguard, and while he's going down, you'll get a clear shot at that bastard."

Card could have smiled. Instead he gave Howard a serious look, it was time to reel him in. "I don't know, Bro. This is serious stuff. You ever shot a man before?"

"Course I have!" Howard lied. "But this ain't no man! This is a dirty, fucking animal!"

Card hesitated a moment, weighing it, then looking around to make sure no one was watching, he palmed one of the derringers over to Howard. There were two shots in it, both silver, but one of the bullets had been rigged to misfire so when the derringer was found, they'd know he'd been using silver bullets.

Howard puffed up then and smiled.

"Okay," Card said in a low voice. "We wait until he comes out. Stay close by me; when I make my move, pull your gun out and follow me, and we'll kill those bastards!"

Howard smiled, thinking about Julie. Oh, he was so going to score with that hot little babe!

Sticking close to Card, he gave Julie a wink and mouthed the word 'nasty' to her the next time they passed by her, and she smiled right back at him, not even looking at Card!

The door opened shortly after that and as Steve came down the stairs with his bodyguards, Howard followed Card to the front of the group, Card moving the others out of their way.

"Now!" Card shouted as the other three drew close. Running forward, he shot one of the bodyguards once, and then tackled him.

Howard suddenly found himself with a gun in his hand and a clear shot at Steve, the leader of those filthy lycan bastards! He paused a moment as everything slowed down, thinking suddenly of Julie, naked in his arms. He'd never had a girl that sexy before!

Raising the derringer, he shot Steve right in the chest, the bullet making a hole in his nice white shirt. Pulling the trigger a second time, he frowned as nothing happened.

He heard it then as Steve stumbled back into the other bodyguard—the screaming. People all around him were screaming! Looking to either side, he saw that there were police, guns out, running towards him! Dropping the pistol, he turned to run, looking for Card, who was nowhere in sight.

Just then the hand of the bodyguard on the ground at his feet grabbed his ankle and pulled him down to the ground.

"Somebody call an ambulance!"

"Don't shoot! Don't shoot! We got him!"

Howard felt something sting him in the back, and then passed out as a bolt of electricity surged through his body.

Card ducked around the corner and dove into the back of the car waiting there.

"Is Steve okay?" he asked as they slowly drove off.

"Yeah, he's fine. Boz has already told us he's just hamming it up, playing for the cameras."

"How's Clifford?"

"He's fine; he grabbed that other guy with you. I can't believe you talked him into shooting Steve!"

"Eh, he was hot for Julie, and she's been playing up to me to get me to 'do something' for days now. Howard thought he'd beat me to it and score with her instead."

"Wow, it's already on the news!" said Kyle, the other guy in the car, holding up his cellphone. Sure enough, there was a live feed coming from in front of the TV station.

"Mission accomplished, huh boys?" Card said with a smile and a feeling of satisfaction he hadn't felt in a very long time.

"Oh, yeah. I think Steve is gonna be beyond pleased."

Learning to Fly

The ride back to the ranch was quiet. Sean was too involved in his own thoughts. Peg, Cali, and Estrella were talking about something without using the intercom, and he didn't feel like interfering. Trey and Daelyn were going over a bunch of stuff on 'angle of attack' settings and something called 'autorotation' as she flew, and Sean wasn't really all that interested in that, either.

He just kept coming back to what he'd gotten himself into, and how in the hell had he ended up here. Sure, this was the kind of thing Chad lived for. Steve was as happy as a pig in shit in Washington. Even John had been doing what he'd loved, right up until the end.

An end Sean hadn't been able to do a thing to prevent, either. That bothered him. He'd sent a lot of people off to their deaths, especially back when all of this got started and they'd had to take on often overwhelming odds, but in order to keep things from spiraling out of their hands, they'd had to, no, *he'd* had to, accept that some of the people who were looking up to him like a god were going to die.

For him.

For their people.

For people they didn't even know, but who were they same as they were. But it had been march or die, kill or be killed. He hadn't had much of a choice in the matter, either, with damn near every magic user in the world out for his head.

Now? These djevels, these demons, they weren't gunning for him. It wasn't anything personal. He was just the guy who had the bad luck to be in the right spot at the right time and got awarded the job.

John had died on his watch; hell, he'd died sitting just a few feet away. Had they really needed to go to DC? Would it have made any real difference if they hadn't bothered tracking down that loose end? With the current state of affairs in Germany, odds were the embassy would have been found out anyway. If they hadn't been recalled back to Germany first when everything back there started falling to pieces.

And Alex…well, he wasn't exactly sure how much of the blame he could take for that. Still, it had been a huge failure in their intelligence, their leadership, *his* leadership. He'd *known* they were having problems in DC, he'd seen it with his own two eyes. It should have occurred to him they'd be having those same problems here and he should have ordered measures to be taken.

But the magic users had caved, and everyone was one big happy family now. Well, maybe not happy, but no one was trying to kill each other anymore. So he'd let his guard down. He'd figured that the only enemy he had to worry about now were the djevels coming through the gates.

And now he spent his days dealing with paperwork, approving all these plans for the future, and sitting in meetings with petty bureaucrats who wanted their asses kissed as they refused to do their jobs.

Sean shook his head, not for the first time missing having the First to fall back on. He could have just gone to sleep and let him deal with the whole thing. No doubt he'd have had a way to get that asshole back in line without pissing off the government of Reno.

Yeah, he wasn't looking forward to dealing with that mess. Politics just wasn't his strong point. Maybe he'd call Steve back and let *him* deal with the mayor and the governor. Then he could just go back to killing things and building stuff in his lab. Things he could understand.

"I'm going off for a run," he said as they landed, and as soon as the door opened, he shifted into his lion form and did just that. He hadn't stretched his legs in days. Maybe that would help him clear his head.

"What's with Sean?" Daelyn asked as she shut the engine down, looking back at the others.

"Let's just say the meeting didn't exactly go as planned," Peg said.

"They were rude to him," Cali grumbled.

"I miss being able to kill underlings who don't know their place," Estrella growled.

"Bill?" Daelyn asked, looking at Roxy's father.

"I've worked with those kinds of people for so long, I've become immune to it, and I'm not so sure that's a good thing."

Getting out of the helicopter, Bill went in search of his daughter. He wasn't sure what was up with his son-in-law, but if anybody would know, she would.

Getting out of the helicopter, he went directly to her office.

"Roxy?" he said, stepping inside.

"Claudia already called and filled me in," Roxy said with a sigh. "Where is he?"

"He ran off, said he needed to stretch his legs."

"Sean has got to be the hardest person in the world to piss off, yet they always seem determined to try." She growled then. "Just how bad was it?"

"He told them he was pulling the troops out of Reno and was going to let it fall."

"He told them *that*?"

"Well, I'd say it was more of a heavy-handed warning. But he didn't really seem all that mad, just, well, sad. Apologized for wasting their time, then left."

"What did Cali, Estrella, and Peg do?"

"Cali and Estrella just left. I don't think they were happy with what had been going on either. Peg, however," Bill sighed and then laughed. "Peg told them there'd be a competition tonight to see who got to kill Justin."

"Justin?"

"That was the guy who was doing all the talking about why none of what Sean asked them to do was going to get done."

Roxy shook her head and chuckled. "Wonder if I can get in on that action?"

"Roxy!"

"What?"

"You can't be serious!"

Roxy snorted. "You're not a cop anymore, Dad. The sad truth is, some of these people either need to get out of the way, or be moved out of the way. Is that why you came here? To get me to stop Estrella or Cali from killing him?"

Bill shook his head. "No, it isn't that. Though I will talk with them later."

"Don't waste your time, Dad. They're not going to listen. So why are you here then?"

"We can't just give up on Reno. There are too many people here, and it's too important. We need to at least try and save it."

"And?"

"Could you talk to him? Please, Roxy? It's not like him just to throw up his hands and walk away from something like this."

"It's what happened to his friend, John," Roxy told him. "It's been eating at him for a while. He still feels a lot of guilt for John's death. He's been second-guessing himself a lot over it, too. They were pretty old friends; they went to junior high school together."

"I didn't know."

"No, of course not. Sean doesn't share a lot with anyone beyond me and the others. I'll go talk with him, Dad. You're right; we can't just walk away from Reno. But you might want to warn everyone that if I get him to come back, he's not going to be all nice and polite about it. Heads are definitely going to roll."

"I think there are probably more than a few that need to be moved on." Bill agreed.

"I was thinking more along the lines of what Adam did to that colonel," Roxy said with a laugh. "I may have been pissed as all hell at him for it, but it sure did work."

"It did?"

"Course it did! Adam's the *nice* one! Everyone here has at one point or another seen what Sean's capable of when he's furious! Hell, they even love telling stories about it!"

"But he always acts like such a calm and polite young man," Bill said, shaking his head.

"That's because he is. Right up until he isn't anymore. Now, let me go find him and see what the deal is."

"And Cali and Estrella?"

"I'll deal with it."

"Thanks, Roxy," Bill said, giving his daughter a hug.

"Anytime, Dad."

#

"You doing okay, Hon?" Roxy asked, walking over to Sean as he sat outside in human form, just staring off into the distance. She'd found him about a mile north of the ranch.

"It's getting harder to hold it all together, Rox," he said with a heavy sigh. "Lately I keep asking myself how I ended up with all of this on my shoulders." Sean waved his arm around behind him, indicating the ranch and everything else.

Roxy laughed. "Yeah, it is kind of a lot now, isn't it? We've got what? A couple thousand people living back there at our little compound?"

Sean snorted. "Little, hell. We've got hangers for two dozen helicopters, workshops, and repair shops everywhere. I've lost count of just how many barracks we've got built now. That place isn't a ranch anymore; it's a freaking army base. Did you hear Daelyn and Estrella talking about building a wall?"

Roxy nodded. "Yeah, they came to me after you told them no. They were just a little miffed. Why did you tell them no, anyways?"

Sean shook his head. "We're not going to be here next month."

"We're not?" Roxy said looking a little surprised.

"If that gate opens anywhere near where Deidre's predicting, that'll put us less than a day's march away. Even if they don't know where we are, they're gonna find out soon enough, and we're going to be number one on their hit parade. There's no way we'll be able to hold this place. I've already told Colonel Tibbets that I want him out of Stead by the fourth. His position is even worse than ours."

"What'd Chad say?"

"That I was right. Claudia's going to be pissed; so are most of the lycan clans, I'm guessing. I've decided to tell them all to be ready to evacuate by the fifteenth and to start sending anyone not involved in the fight south to Vegas by the end of this month."

"That's only a few days away."

"Yeah." Sean sighed and nodded. "I know."

Roxy nodded. "Yeah, I'm sure I'm gonna hear them grumbling about this one." She stepped over in front of him then and dropped down into his lap, looking into his eyes. "And that's why you're the one in charge, Hon. Because you know what needs to be done, and you're *doing* it. You're not feeding everyone a line of bullshit about how it's all going to be alright. You're preparing for the worst, and you're kicking ass when it needs kicked."

"I know, I know," Sean sighed and looked back at her. "Still, I wish I had the First here to back me up sometimes."

"I'm sure he's very proud of just how well you're dealing with everything."

Sean laughed. "You should hear some of our arguments now. He didn't want to send Raban to Munich. Hell, he didn't want to appoint anybody to take over the mess there."

"Why not?"

"He told me he had it covered, and when I asked them what that meant, he told me it wasn't any of my concern."

"And you of course made it your concern," Roxy said with a snicker.

"Damn, I hate it when he won't tell me what he's up to, and I unloaded on him in front of everybody. I told him his biggest problem is that he still thinks he's a god at times, and he needs to hear from us 'mere mortals' because some of his ideas are just stupid."

"What'd he say to that?"

"He reminded me that I'm a god now, too," Sean said and looked embarrassed.

"What about the others?"

Sean grinned. "We've both told them they're not allowed to take sides in our little dustups."

Roxy raised an eyebrow. "Oh?"

"The First doesn't take well to rebellion in the ranks, and after having him in my head for a year, I can't say I disagree with him. He may be a self-centered ass at times, but he's still better than damn near all of them."

"Well, regardless of your little fights, he still sent Raban in, and from what I've heard from Jack via his intelligence briefs and Estrella, it's made a huge change in morale for the people fighting there."

"I just wish we could do something about Berlin."

"Didn't you just say the First said he had a plan for that?"

"Yeah." Sean shook his head and gave her a worried look. "And that's what bothers me. He can be cold at times, Rox, damn cold. And calculating. He really does have the whole god thing down."

"You're afraid you're going to become like him, aren't you?"

Sean nodded. "There are times I think I already am."

Roxy wrapped her arms around him and laid her head on his shoulder. "A man's gotta do what a man's gotta do. I've heard that expression so many times from my father whenever there was something going on in Vegas he had to deal with that he wasn't looking forward to."

"So you're saying I need to become like him?" Sean grumbled and put his arms around her.

"You adopted him as your father, Hon. I got to know him fairly well back when he lived in your head. We all like him, he was kind and considerate, and I think he really does love you like a son."

"Yeah, but that's not who he is now; he's gotten a lot harder these last few weeks. Meaner, tougher."

Roxy nodded her head as she leaned into him. "He's gotta do the bad stuff now, like it or not. And so do you."

Sean sighed again and dropped his head. "And that's the part I hate. I gotta become just as big a bastard as he is."

"Oh, I wouldn't worry about that, he's had what? A hundred thousand years to work on it? You've got a long way to go before you'll be anywhere near as good!" Roxy said with a small laugh.

"You're not making me feel better about it, Rox," Sean growled half-heartedly.

Roxy pulled back and looked him in the eyes. "I married a lion, Sean. A *lion*. A big, buff, dominant, do it my way or I'll pound you into the fucking highway *lion*, named Sean Valens. The First is right; you *are* a god now, Sean."

Roxy put her finger on his mouth as he opened it to protest, stopping him.

"You can't deny it any more than I can. I sure got one hell of a lot more than I expected when I tracked you down that afternoon after I stopped you from killing Dean. And I haven't regretted a single moment. Why? Because you are who you are, and you're mine. I've seen you at your best, and I've seen you at your worst. Well, a week from now the doors to hell are going to open up, and they're doing it in our very own backyard. Like it or not, we need you, and we need you at your *worst*.

"We need, no fuck that, *I need* for my lion, my *god*, the one who takes me to bed and makes me his every night, to get his head in the game and punish the ever loving hell out of those fucking demons for coming here and thinking they have any right at all to mess with that which is *his!* Have I made myself clear?"

Sean looked up at Roxy; she was all but growling now. If she'd been in her hybrid form, he was sure she would have been. Grabbing her head, he pulled her close and kissed her. He had no idea what he'd done in life to deserve a woman like her. All he knew was he was glad he did.

Breaking the kiss, he smiled at her as she gasped and melted against him. He then shifted into his hybrid form. She was right, he was a god, and these were his people.

It was time to start acting like one.

"We need to go see Arthur," he growled.

"Why?"

"Because I need to give him his orders," Sean chuckled, "along with the rest of the magic users and everyone else. You're right, I'm a god. It's time to make sure everyone knows."

"Should I alert Dae to get one of the helicopters ready?"

"No, we'll take her 'Cuda. It'll be just you, her, Jo, and me. Like old times," Sean said with a snort.

"What about Cali and the others?"

Sean snorted. "I got the distinct impression they had something else planned for tonight."

"And here I thought you'd missed it."

"A good husband knows when to *not* pay attention to whatever mayhem his wives are planning."

Shifting back into his lion form, Sean raced Roxy back to the ranch. He lost of course, but that just meant he got to enjoy the view.

Storm Warnings

"Sean, to what do I owe the pleasure?" Arthur said, coming over and shaking hands with Sean as he entered the room. "Jo, always nice to see you!" he said, giving his niece a hug. "Daelyn, Roxy, good to see you both as well," he added, giving each of them a hug, too.

"I'm guessing this isn't a social call," Arthur said as he motioned to the couch and sat down himself, "seeing as you're not in your human form?"

Sean nodded and sat down with his wives. "Apparently a lot of people are getting too familiar with it and starting to think I'm just some young man they don't have to pay attention to."

"My, that doesn't sound good," Arthur said, his expression turning serious. "Surely I'm not on that list?"

"No, you're not, but," Sean gave him a wry grin, "the time has come to talk of many things, of shoes and ships and sealing wax…and I'm about to be a bastard and start ordering you all around like a king."

"Are you really sure you want to start doing that? There's going to be a lot of resistance, Sean. A lot of the magic users around here aren't your biggest fans after what you did to them last year."

"And that's why I'm going around like this now. To remind everyone who and what I am, and that if I have to be a complete asshole, I can and will be. This isn't something I want to do, Arthur. But it's something I definitely have to do, because quite simply, I'm not so sure most of you are going to live through what's coming if I don't put my hand in."

"Why do you say that?"

"How many of your people have you evacuated from Reno? Fifty percent? Seventy?"

Arthur looked at him, blinking. "We haven't evacuated *anyone*. Is there a reason?"

"Arthur, right now I'm considering not even wasting the time and effort to defend it."

Sean didn't miss the shocked expression on Arthur's face. "You're not? Why?"

"Because no matter what I do, Reno *is going to fall*. We just don't have the ability to stop its destruction. The city is too big, has no natural defenses, and very few manmade ones. So I'm ordering all the mages to send their families south. Vegas is probably a safe bet. I only want those here who are involved in the fight, so when things do turn bad, we can get them out of here quickly."

Arthur nodded slowly. "When you put it like that, it's hard to disagree…"

"Though some people will," Jolene said snarkily.

Arthur laughed. "Yes, Jolene, some people always will. But I don't think anyone has realized that things are so dire."

Sean sighed. "Mainly we've been keeping those opinions quiet, and just hoping the changing climate with all the military here would encourage folks to leave. I didn't think I'd be the one to have to tell them it's time to go."

"And what changed that?"

"The actions of some of the people working for the city who are supposed to be building our defenses. I guess I shouldn't blame them; all of this is so far beyond anything they've ever experienced before. So of course they don't believe what's coming."

"So you're taking over."

Sean nodded. "I'm probably going to declare martial law and appoint myself military governor or something. I'd go for king," Sean said with a grin, "but I suspect most folks wouldn't go along with that."

Arthur laughed. "Yes, I think it's been bred into most Americans to resist *that* idea. I'll call a meeting of the Sapientia local council immediately and tell them. How soon do you want everyone out?"

"By the fourth, but sooner would be better. There's one other thing I want to show you. Do you have a map?"

"Actually, I have several. I'm not exactly a fan of the online ones. Too old school, I guess."

Getting up, Arthur led Sean over to a shelf, where he pulled out a Rand McNally for Nevada.

"Great," Sean said, opening it up. He went through it and found the place he was looking for. It was south of Minden, on highway 88.

"Okay," Sean said, marking a small spot. "There's a safe house here. Only you, me, and my wife Estrella know of it. This is for *your* use only." Sean wrote down the few notes Sawyer had given him on how the safe houses worked, along with the exact address. "Commit this to memory, then burn it. Don't tell *anybody* about it unless you're sending them there."

"What they don't know they can't share, right?"

Sean nodded. "Exactly so. I'm going to give Joseph a different one for his people."

"What about the other councils?"

"The Sorceress Guild, but that's it."

"Why them?"

"Because Deanna is my mother-in-law?" Sean said with a smile.

"And they've always been good to you," Arthur agreed.

"That, too. Okay, the next order of business. Starting this weekend, I want the magic users who are working with us to start bunking with their respective units."

"Are you sure about that, Sean? Sleeping with them?"

Sean snorted. "I'm not asking them to sleep together in the same bed; that's up to them. But they need to start living with their teams. We don't have the time or the means to keep flying them out to meet their team each time something comes up. It's time for them to become a part of those teams, and that means living together.

"That needs to start immediately."

"I have to warn you, you'll probably lose several magic users."

Roxy spoke up, "Tell them they're going to be living with the only armed people who can protect them. See if that changes their minds."

Jolene nodded. "Really, Arthur. They've been working with these teams for weeks, if not months. I'd think they'd be over any prejudices by now."

Arthur smiled. "I think it's more a matter of them not wanting to give up their current level of luxury. None of us are very good at 'roughing it'. Even I have grown rather fond of the pleasures that living in a nice house bring."

"Well, they might want to get used ta the idea," Daelyn said with a snicker. "Because we're all gonna end up refugees here soon enough. And even after the war's won, I suspect we're all gonna find that a lot of our homes are gone."

"As much as I'd like to disagree with you, I suspect you're right," Arthur said with a heavy sigh.

"When I traveled as a young man, I saw far too often what conflict did to a town or city, and we're going to have a full-blown war coming through."

Arthur paused a moment.

"So you *really* don't think you're going to be able to save Reno?"

Sean shook his head.

"Could you at least *try*? That's a lot of people, Sean. Even if you can only put off the inevitable for a little while, every day will count."

"I'll see, Arthur. A lot is going to depend on what happens when I go in there and lay down the law tomorrow. If I have to kill people to get them to comply, that kind of defeats the whole purpose of trying to save them."

Arthur snorted. "Maybe you should think of it as denying the demons a food source?"

Jolene blinked. "I had no idea you could be so cold, Arthur."

"Hard times call for hard measures, Jolene, and I'm starting to worry that maybe I've been ignoring the coming realities. There are things worse than death, and I would say having your soul eaten qualifies, wouldn't you?"

"Yes, Uncle," Jolene said with a sigh. "I would."

"You know, I never thought I'd miss the days when all we were worried about was fighting the magic users," Roxy said with a laugh.

"Life is funny that way," Arthur agreed.

"Okay, here's the last order of business before we go."

Arthur looked at Sean curiously. "Yes?"

"We need someone to organize Sapientia to fight in this war. I'm not just talking about the Reno council; I'm talking about all the councils. I don't care how you do it, but I need someone I, or my generals, can talk with about deploying your people. Not just here in Reno, but anywhere in the country. I need a liaison; I need your version of a general for the war."

"That's a pretty big order, Sean."

"I know, but once you admit Reno will fall, you realize we're going to be having problems all over the country. So if I'm going to be able to get any help from the mages, I need a single point of contact. I'm hoping I only need one, someone who can deal with all the different councils, major and minor. But if I have to get someone from each of the councils, I will."

"And where do you want this person?"

"I want them sitting at my conference table. I want them to take part in our planning, and for them to know everything we know as soon as we know it. It's not going to be an easy job for whoever ends up with it. But I need someone who, if they make a promise, it'll be carried out or heads will literally roll."

"Now *that* is a tall order. But it is one we've been anticipating. I'll talk with Duncan."

Sean smiled and, standing up, he bent over and shook hands with Arthur. "Thanks, Arthur, for everything. I'm not sure when we'll see each other again. In a few days the main gateway opens, and I suspect we'll both be far too busy for social calls or personal meetings."

"I'm sure you're right. Good luck, Sean. I'll get it taken care of."

Sean opened the door and showed Roxy, Jolene, and Daelyn out. Starting out after them, he stopped and looked back at Arthur.

"Just for the record, the oldest of us are over two hundred thousand years old. We started out around the same time as modern humans, and had a lot to do with the extinction of the Neanderthals. We ruled for tens of thousands of years, and ran some of the bloodiest wars you could possibly imagine, and we did it all for sport. We raised armies of millions and pitted them against each other until none were left.

"And we did it for nothing more than bragging rights. That's why the lions refuse to rule the world ever again. It was foolish, and it was stupid. We had all the power in the world, and precious little wisdom to temper it. Now I wasn't there for all of that, and I'd like to believe we've moved beyond that as our wisdom and experience has grown with time."

"They're coming back, aren't they?"

Sean sighed. "I think this war is going to determine that. We're lions. We're possessive. Territory is *everything*. And dammit, this planet is *ours*. Just because we handed it over to you humans to run it, don't ever think it doesn't still belong to us."

"Why are you telling me this?"

"Because after all the teasing I've done this last year, I thought you deserved to know why we're doing this. To know that we're committed."

Sean left the room then, closing the door behind him.

"Did that really answer any questions?" James asked, looking at Arthur.

"Actually, yes, I think it did, James. Now summon the council, I need to call Duncan and get things rolling."

Sean's visit with Joseph wasn't much different than the one he'd had with Arthur. Only two things had gone differently; Joseph had already started evacuating his people, and he didn't need a safe house for emergencies, he already had several of his own.

Sean also didn't make his little speech; he figured Arthur would share that on his own eventually.

Deanna was quite grateful. They didn't have all that many families in the Sorceress guild, a lot of the sorceresses came from other councils when they started to chafe at the restrictions many of them still put on women.

There were also no complaints at the idea of bunking with the units they were working with. To be fair, a lot of the sorceresses were already doing that, having brought their mates or partners with them.

"So, Claudia's?" Daelyn asked as they left the Sorceress Guild.

"Yeah, that sounds about right," Sean said with a sigh. "Do you think I need to talk to your uncle or the other leaders of the Carson City dwarven hall?"

"Nah, they'll just seal it all up and put guards on the entrances. Ain't no djevel or demon out there that's ever gonna break into a dwarven hall. They've been beefing up the defenses since you ordered all those swords. You gotta remember, we've been down this road before."

"Fifteen hundred years ago," Roxy pointed out.

"Two things dwarves never forget, Rox: Friends and enemies, as well as how to deal with both."

"Well, considering how you all reacted to Sean, I can believe it."

Sean thought about that while they made the quick drive to Claudia's, trying to think if there was anybody else he needed to have a talk with. Maybe he should send some folks to Sacramento and some of the other cities to warn them what was coming.

"We're here!" Daelyn said, sliding the car to a stop.

"I noticed," Sean said. Getting out, he helped Jolene out of the back as Claudia came walking up to them quickly.

"Wow, I thought you'd make me come to your office!" Sean said with a grin.

Claudia snorted. "I've learned better than that, thank you. So what brings you here? And why are you going around furry?"

"I think I've been going too easy on a lot of people. The time to crack the whip is here, and if people see a big ass lion instead of a wet-behind-the-ears college kid, I think they'll start to realize I mean business."

"I've been following orders!" Claudia said, looking a little nervous for a change.

Sean nodded. "I know, but I'm still going to be a bit of an asshole. I want you to evacuate everyone who isn't necessary to the war south to Vegas."

"So you really are giving up on Reno?"

"Sooner or later, Reno is going to fall. You know that, Claudia."

"Still, I was hoping we'd make the attempt. The longer they're attacking Reno, the less they're attacking someplace else."

Sean nodded, conceding the point. "I think a lot of it is going to depend on tomorrow's meeting with the mayor."

"We're having a meeting tomorrow?" Claudia asked, looking surprised.

"Let's just say I'm expecting several irate phone calls come the morning."

"So your wives really are going..." Claudia stopped when Sean raised a hand.

"I have no idea about anything they're planning, and I prefer it that way."

"Then what makes you so sure?"

Sean snorted. "Cali and Estrella were both raised to kill things and have little patience with disrespect. I don't think I need any kind of crystal ball, do you?"

Claudia shook her head with a grin. "Can't say as they don't have it coming, either. Honestly, I was surprised you didn't rip a few throats out then and there."

Sean nodded. "Yeah. Maybe I should have. Look, I have the location of a couple of safe houses I want to share with you. You can't tell anyone about it unless you're sending them there."

"Do you really think we'll need them?"

Sean shrugged. "I'm not sure. I think when Reno does fall, things are going to be really confused, and until we figure out how to deal with it, there's probably going to be a lot of possessed people and disguised djevels running around."

"We can always go to the dwarves," Claudia said with a nod towards Daelyn. "In fact, we were already discussing that with Roloff. Once they have to seal up their mountain, it'll be beneficial if they have some lycan warriors to help them."

"That's a good idea," Sean conceded. "Still, you're probably going to need a few places for people or things you don't want to expose them too."

"Well, I won't turn down anything that might help." Claudia pondered a moment. "What about your helicopter repair facility and all those mechanics you've got up there?"

"We need them too much to send them all away yet," Sean admitted, "but I don't think we're still going to be there a month from now. Once it looks like we'll be moving, we'll send them out first."

"Any idea where?"

"Well, if we end up making a stand at Reno, I'll probably send them south to the airport. A lot of it is going to depend on just what kind of a fight we've gotten ourselves into at that point. We're still dealing with a lot of unknowns here. We think they'll form up raiding groups and travel in columns, like that first big group that got out did. But…" Sean shrugged again.

Claudia nodded. "Well, come on in and you can show me where those safe houses are. After that, we can talk about tomorrow. I can tell you the mayor's just a little bit scared right now, and if Cali and Estrella do what Peg threatened," Claudia snorted, "she's going to be in a complete panic."

"Yeah, I hate the idea that I have to play the heavy. I'm sure she's never going to look at me the same way again."

"You say that like it's a bad thing." Roxy snickered.

"Roxy has a point. You're not one of them; honestly, you never were. Now you're someone special. They need to remember that, and act accordingly."

Sean looked at Claudia in surprise.

"What?" she said, looking back at him. "You of all people should know that I know exactly who and what you are. You may drive me crazy at times, or piss me off, but I've learned enough to know you are what you claim to be, and you seem to have some sort of mystical connection and know things the rest of us don't.

"Besides, you've always played fair with me and all the rest, even though you made it perfectly clear with Michael that you didn't have to."

"Yeah, I'm sorry it came to that, but he wasn't taking care of his pack, and he was an asshole."

"You won't get any arguments from me on that!" Claudia laughed. "I was going to undercut him and take it out from under him. Putting your friend Chad in charge was a good move. He's a solid alpha, and he got that pack cleaned up in record time."

"And he married your daughter," Roxy added with a laugh.

"All the more proof that he's the perfect wolf for the job," Claudia agreed. "Wolves have been putting the moves on her for years in the hopes of getting a leg up in my pack. I'd brought her with me to meet him, figuring I'd get a move on *his* pack, and what does she do? Dumps her own mother and mates with him!"

"You do know they knew each other before they met?"

Claudia blinked. "What? How?"

"World of Warcraft, online. Apparently Chad, Max, and even Sean here were all in the same online group."

"Guild, it's called a guild," Sean said, trying not to laugh at the look of surprise on Claudia's face. "I think Chad figured it out almost immediately, and told her when you weren't around. So it kind of greased the skids a little."

Claudia growled, "I knew letting her get that computer was a bad idea!"

"Oh, I don't know, I think he would have still won her over," Roxy said, grinning. "Chad's a lot more aggressive about going after what he wants than most wolves."

"I've noticed. I think he's starting to give *my* pack the eye."

"Nah, you're his mother-in-law," Sean said. "He actually likes you, but he definitely wants to learn every last one of your secrets so he can steal 'em. He wasn't born a wolf, remember."

"Maybe not, but he took to it like a fish to water. Boy's a natural. If it wasn't for this damn war, I bet he could have extended the western pack all the way down into Sacramento."

They came into Claudia's office at that point, and Sean took a moment to show her the two safe houses he'd marked out for her and her pack.

"Did you give Chad any?"

"One, but he's got a couple of his own he's developing, too."

"Who'd you have set these up for you?"

Sean grinned. "If you wanted something done in secret, on the sly, and without anyone, including the authorities to know, who would you go to?"

"Sawyer."

"Yup, so when this is all said and done, remember to be nice to him. I gotta say, he and his family, or 'line' as they like to call it, have been lifesavers."

"Are you going to give any of these out to any of the other lycan clans?"

"I'm going to give Clyde some. With all the scouting work his people have been doing, I suspect they're going to need it. But I don't think the others need them. I figure they'll be in the thick of it with the army and will retreat with us when the time comes.

"Which reminds me. Call a meeting of the fellowship. This is going to be the last one we have, because once the main gateway opens, I don't think any of us are going to have the time to get together safely again."

Claudia nodded. "You got it, Sean." She paused then and looked around the room. "You know, I'm gonna miss this place; took me twenty years to build it."

"You can always rebuild after the war's over," Jolene pointed out.

Claudia shook her head. "No. No, I don't think a place like this is gonna work in the world we'll be living in then."

Sean looked at his watch; it was getting late.

"Well, we need to get back to the ranch. Until tomorrow, Claudia."

"Have a good night, Sean. And ask them not to get too messy."

Sean snorted. "Like they'd listen."

The Formula of Fear

"You know you did not have to come with us," Cali said to Peg, who was driving.

"Someone had to drive. Besides, I know the systems they use around here, and I also know the city."

"Sheila could have driven us; she knows the alarms, as well."

Peg rolled her eyes as she turned off the highway. "Cali, I was *there*, I'm not letting the two of you have all of the fun by yourselves! Just because I'm not a cold-blooded killer like the two of you doesn't mean I can't help."

"Cold-blooded killer? Really, Peg?" Estrella asked with a sharp look.

"I meant it as a compliment," Peg said, grinning. "Me and Sheila, we've done a few things around town, but I just don't have that extra whatever-it-is you two have to put the bastards in the ground like they really deserve."

"I do not know that it is such a bad thing," Cali said with a smile. "Sheila confided in me what you both did to that one merchant. That was far better than killing him would ever have been."

"Oh?" Estrella looked over at Cali. "What'd they do?"

"They turned him into a fox boy sex toy and sold him off to someone who uses them quite rudely."

"Why'd they do that?"

"Because he was the one who sold Sheila to my dad," Peg said with a hint of anger, "as well as bought and sold a lot of other lycans, most of them into very nasty conditions they didn't survive."

Estrella's eyes widened slightly. "Cali, love? Perhaps we're being a bit hasty; maybe we should let Peg deal with this one."

"Oh, no! I told the mayor and the rest he was as good as dead."

"You *told* them?"

"Random violence doesn't inspire the same kind of fear as a good old targeted killing," Peg said. "I learned that one from Cali."

Estrella looked at Cali, who smiled and nodded. "It is nice to be appreciated."

"I keep forgetting you're a professional," Estrella admitted. "I'm just used to killing people because they upset me one time too many."

"He only insulted Sean the once, you know," Cali pointed out.

"Still one time too many," Estrella said with an evil grin.

"Agreed."

"Hey, got my vote!" Peg chimed in. "And is it my imagination, or are there a lot of people on the street for this time of night?"

"Apparently they took your warning to heart," Estrella said, sliding down a little in her seat.

"Let us turn left up ahead and see how many streets they are covering," Cali said.

Nodding, Peg did as Cali told her. They drove down two more blocks, and suddenly the pedestrian traffic completely disappeared.

"Go one more and turn down it," Cali directed.

"So what's the plan?" Estrella asked.

"We find a safe spot to park and walk."

"There were a lot of people out there, Cali."

Cali smiled. "Yes, there were. So we grab three, render them unconscious, and then our Peg here casts an illusion on us and we just walk on by."

"Won't they have signs and counter-signs?"

Peg snorted. "These are cops, Stell, not military."

"Well, that's sloppy."

"And we shall be grateful for it," Cali said with a smile.

Peg parked in a driveway with another car already in it, putting a silence spell on it so no one would hear the sound of the doors opening and closing. She'd already put an illusion on the license plates back at the ranch, so the number on them wouldn't lead back to them.

"Follow me," Cali whispered, leading them across the street and into the backyard of the house there. All three of them were wearing dark clothing, gloves, and had stocking caps to pull down if necessary. While Peg and Estrella didn't really stand out, Cali's unique looks most definitely would if they were seen.

She then led them over a few yards to a spot where they were able to observe the next street from cover.

"I don't see anyone," Estrella whispered.

"Me neither," Peg agreed.

"Okay, at a walk, we cross," Cali said.

"Shouldn't we go one at a time?" Peg asked.

"That would look suspicious, would it not?" Cali grinned.

Peg had to nod in agreement as they all crossed together, and then ducked into the next backyard. Working their way through to the other side, they could see that this street was being patrolled by several men and women in plainclothes.

"This one is going to be a bit tougher; they're too spread out to take one out without the others seeing."

Peg looked up and down the street. There weren't any streetlights, and most of the houses had all of the lights off, considering the lateness of the hour.

"I can put a spell on me and Estrella that'll make us look like house cats, but we'll have to shift into our animal forms."

"I think I might be a bit big to pass for a house cat," Estrella said with a snicker.

"Size doesn't matter."

"Where have I heard *that* before?" Cali wondered.

Peg stifled a laugh, and Estrella had to put both hands over her mouth.

"Can you cast that on me?" Cali asked.

Peg shook her head. "You'd look like a cat walking on its hind legs, and it would still walk like a human."

Cali took a second look around. "It's okay, we'll meet behind that house with the tree in the front yard."

"You sure?" Peg asked, worried.

Cali smiled and nodded.

Peg shrugged. "Shift, Stell."

The moment Estrella shifted, Peg cast the spell on her, then cast it again on herself, shifting immediately into her fox form.

"Good, now go," Cali said as she watched the two cats move quickly out into the front yard and across the street. Estrella, being much larger, moved faster, but the illusion made it look as if she was running and Peg was chasing her.

Dropping down into a crouch, Cali moved quickly in a line straight towards one of the cars parked in the driveway of the house next door, as they were closest and were well hidden in shadows.

The lack of light made most of the shadows fairly dark, but there was enough to keep them from being large or solid. But she knew the biggest part of not being seen was to not look like something that would catch the eye.

Quickly moving to the side of a car in the street, she crouched down by the tire, but placed her arm on the side, bent at an odd angle with her thumb folded and fingers pointed. It wasn't much, but the jagged black shape would just make the human eye think they were seeing an odd shadow, not a person.

Keeping her eyes moving, she waited until the two nearest people were looking away from the street before her, then she dashed across and went prone on the ground in the strip between the street and the sidewalk in the shadow of a large mailbox. If the people further back had seen anything, they discounted it because the closer ones hadn't said anything.

She waited a moment, and then carefully moved over to the car in the driveway when no one was paying too much attention, then ducked around behind the house to meet up with Peg and Estrella.

"How'd you do that?" Estrella asked.

"Practice. Now, let us continue."

They had to be a bit more careful, moving closer, because the next street had a dozen people on it. Their target lived in a house on the other side.

"They are certainly taking this seriously," Peg said looking back and forth along the street.

"I am surprised that I do not see any magical traps or wards," Cali said after a few minutes of scanning the street.

"There aren't any magic users working for the city, Cali."

"True, but they have obviously taken your threat seriously, and they know *we* have magic users. They know magic users exist. They most likely could have called one of the councils and hired one to help with this."

"Which means?"

Estrella gave Cali a thoughtful look. "Which means there is a chance he isn't even in that house. That they've moved him someplace else, and this is either a ruse or a trap."

"If it's a trap, they'll have put something nasty in his bedroom," Peg surmised. "Let's circle the block, I have an idea."

Cali nodded. "Lead on." Peg led them carefully from backyard to backyard, down past where the stakeout was taking place. They carefully crossed over two streets, and then started back down on the other side.

"What are we looking for?" Estrella asked, noticing Peg was checking the streets to either side of the section of houses they were cutting through.

"A van. Like the one John used."

"I haven't seen any drones," Cali said, glancing upwards.

"I haven't either," Peg said, but a few minutes later she pointed down the block. Sure enough, there was a fairly large and nondescript van. It was two blocks over from the house, so there were very few people on the street.

"I think that's their command post. If they have a trap in the room, it'll be triggered from there."

"Well, what do you say we go take a look?" Cali asked, grinning.

"I have a couple of sleep wands," Peg said, "but we need to make sure we don't alert anyone on the street."

"They parked the van on the far side, and all their watchers are on the near side. I do not think we'll have much of a problem," Cali said. Taking over, she led them back a bit away from the watchers, then crossed the street so they'd have an easier time coming up on the van.

"It's almost three; if he's not in there, I don't know how we're going to get him tonight," Estrella grumbled in a low voice as they finally reached a spot by a house less than twenty feet from the van.

"First things first," Cali said. "Peg, go sleep everyone in the van, then do your cat trick, go get the car, and meet us on the street behind this one."

"Got it," Peg said, and taking a quick look to be sure the coast was clear, she ran up to the van, stuck the wand between the doors, and fired it off. She then cast her illusion spell on herself and ran off.

"Wait here until I call you," Cali said and carefully snuck out to the van. The side door was locked, but picking it only took a minute. Stepping inside, she reached up and turned off the door light. There were two men inside, both sound asleep in their seats. Across from them were a number of monitors that showed a couple of rooms inside a house.

It only took her a minute to figure out which one was the main bedroom. There was a large red mushroom shaped button under it, and she could easily guess what that was for. Looking back to Estrella, she waved her forward.

"Close the door, carefully," Cali whispered. "We don't want to wake them up yet."

"Well it looks like it is a trap," Estrella whispered back. "So now what?"

"Look for any notes, or a logbook. Maybe they wrote down where he is? We must be quick. They'll be in a normal sleep soon; any loud noise will wake them."

Estrella nodded and went up to the driver's compartment to see what was there, while Cali looked through the notebook one of them had been writing things in. She found a number of notes on how they'd set up the cameras inside and the sleeping gas pacification bombs they'd put in the main bedroom, as well as several more in the rest of the home. There were more notes, mostly just a log of what they'd seen on the cameras outside the house, and a status written down every half hour.

Setting it down in disgust, she turned to Estrella in the front.

"Find anything?"

"A bunch of those little yellow sticky papers with numbers scrawled on them."

"Really?" Cali said looking interesting. "Any of them have the name Justin on them?"

"One of them."

"Great, grab it and let's get out of here."

"What is it?" Estrella asked Cali as they got out and she carefully closed the door, then knocked on it once as they ran back into the shadows. It wouldn't do for someone to find the two guys sleeping inside. Hopefully one of them would wake up at her knock and they'd just be embarrassed and not tell anyone.

Cali glanced at the note. "It's a phone number."

"What good is that?"

"I know someone we can call who can tell us where it is."

"You do?"

Cali nodde., "John's girlfriend, Cenna. If she can't find it, I'm sure she knows someone who can."

"He's where?" Peg asked as she drove off with the other two.

"Cenna told me his cellphone appears to be at a hotel over on Stardust and Elgin."

Peg nodded. "I know where that is."

"You do?"

Peg grinned. "Let's just say it's a popular place for guys to take their girlfriends, and back before I met Sean, I was a *very* rebellious little girl."

"Now we just need to figure out what room he's in," Estrella said. "Any ideas?"

"Let me think about it after I've seen what the place looks like," Cali said, her brows furrowed as she considered this new problem.

"Just find out which room the police are in, and he'll be next door, I bet," Peg said. "I'm just surprised they're investing this much money and effort in protecting him."

"They are most likely afraid they may be next."

"All the more reason to make him first then, isn't it?" Estrella said with a snicker, "Fear always keeps the lesser races in line."

"Lesser races?" Peg asked, looking at her.

Estrella had the good graces to look embarrassed. "In my defense, I did just spend a millennium trapped in the Onderwereld."

"And the First is your father," Peg added with a grin.

"Yeah, that too."

It didn't take them much longer to get to the hotel. Peg did a slow circuit in the car, while Cali and Estrella looked out the windows.

"I'm surprised they didn't put him in a casino," Peg observed as she finally found a place to park on the next street over.

"From what I have learned from Claudia about casinos," Cali said as they all got out of the car, "they do not like having the police around."

"What? Are they afraid of getting caught cheating or something?"

Cali shook her head. "Casinos are in business to make money. They don't want anything getting in the way of that. Like, say, the police arresting people for things their own security would simply take them back to their rooms for."

Peg nodded. "Makes sense I guess."

"That and they don't want people getting killed in their hotels. It is, as Claudia says, 'Bad for Business"."

Both Peg and Estrella snickered at that.

Cali stopped as she had a thought, then turned to Peg, who was looking at her.

"Yes?" Peg asked.

"Do you think you could still cast an illusion on us to make us look like police officers?"

Peg nodded. "Sure, easily. Why?"

Cali smiled. "We just walk in the front door, and as we walk by the desk, we ask what room are the other officers are in."

"And our target is right next door." Peg grinned. "I like it. Give me a moment, stand still, both of you."

Estrella and Cali waited patiently as Peg closed her eyes and made some motions with her arms while mumbling something softly. Then she did a twirl on one foot, and when she stopped, there was a much older man standing there in a cheap suit, with a badge on a cord around his neck. Cali and Estrella were both also men now, but they were dressed in regular patrol uniforms for the Reno Police Department.

"Now, let's go inside," Peg said, in a much different voice.

"Lead on," Estrella said, noticing that her voice was much different now as well.

With a nod of her head, Peg led them inside the lobby for the hotel. Except for the young man behind the counter, there was no one else there.

"Evening, Officers," he said, giving them a quick glance before returning to looking at something on his smartphone.

Peg turned to Cali., "Sheldon, what room are they in again?"

Cali just shrugged.

"Great, run out to the car and grab the folder," Peg said with a heavy sigh.

"Rooms two-eleven and two-thirteen," the young man behind the desk answered without even looking up. "Stairs are at the end of the hallway."

"Thanks," Peg said with a wave and led them down the hallway to the stairs.

"That was easier than I thought it would be," Estrella admitted in a low voice as they went up the stairs.

"Are there any cameras here?" Cali asked.

"Yes, but they're not seeing us," Peg told her.

Looking down the hallway, they didn't see anyone keeping watch.

"How much longer will this illusion last?"

"About two minutes. Or until you touch anything grounded."

"Thanks. Now wait here," Cali said, putting a hand on Peg's shoulder.

Peg nodded and gulped. Robbing people was one thing; killing them, well, as much as she felt this guy had to go, she didn't want to be there when he went.

Cali led off down the hallway, with Estrella close behind. For all that they looked like a couple of uniformed officers, they still moved as silently as they ever did, the items on their utility belts not making any noise.

When Cali reached room two eleven, she stopped a moment and listened, while Estrella sniffed the air. She could hear several men and women inside talking. Looking at Estrella, she shook her head. Estrella nodded and held up her hands with six fingers up. Cali thought about that; six wouldn't be too much trouble if worse came to worse.

Moving to the next door, she stopped and listened. Even with her sensitive ears, it took a moment to hear the soft snoring inside. She looked at Estrella, who nodded and held up one finger.

Turning back to the door, Cali pulled out a piece of very intelligent plastic. It looked like a credit card, but this wonderful little magical device slid around the door jamb as she worked it in. Then with a squeeze at the right spot, it flowed around and under the latch as it became almost liquid at the end.

Once she'd worked it into the right spot, she stopped squeezing it, and the plastic returned to its flat shape with the single bend, forcing the striker back into the door as it did so.

Pulling out a second card, she worked this one around the door just above the deadbolt. Squeezing that one turned the bottom edge into an incredibly sharp magical knife, and with a little bit of muscle, she sliced through the deadbolt without any difficulty, pushing the door open slowly.

Scanning the room, they both saw their target, Justin, was asleep in the bed. But the door to the adjoining room was open. Thankfully someone, probably Justin, had turned the radio on and tuned it to static. The low noise was quite good at covering the muffled conversations of the officers in the next room.

Recovering her cards, Cali put them away, then carefully turned the deadbolt so it went back into the door. She added a couple of drops of a 'magical' epoxy she'd bought at the hardware store on the cut end after she pried the other piece out of the slot, and put it back together. Once it hardened, unless you looked at it, you'd never know it was cut.

They both stepped inside the room carefully then, Estrella slowly closing the door almost all the way. The metal door jamb must have been grounded, because Cali noticed her illusion was gone, though Estrella's persisted. Dropping down to her hands and knees, she took out a small mirror to peer around the open door to see what she was dealing with.

There was an officer sitting there with a smartphone, reading something on it and looking up occasionally. From his vantage point he could see most of the bed, but definitely not all of it.

She held up a hand to wave Estrella back. The moment he looked up again, she prepared herself, and when he looked down, she quietly moved across the open doorway. Staying low, she crawled around the bed to the far side, out of sight of the watchman. Looking back at Estrella again, she motioned for her to wait as she got out a rolled-up piece of cloth. Unrolling it carefully, Cali looked at the six long needles, each of which was in a special, well-protected pocket. They were each coated with a poison. Three were instant, the other three were not, and one of those had some very nasty side effects before it killed you, slowly.

If she killed him instantly, he'd stop snoring, and someone would come in to investigate. So one of the slow ones it was. But making this look as natural as possible was in order here. Besides, he hadn't quite done anything that required him to suffer, just to die.

Pulling out one of the two, she made her choice, then slid her hands under the bed covers, gently touching his arm, looking for a spot that wasn't protected by clothing. Once she found that, she brought the needle close, withdrawing her other hand to keep from accidentally stabbing herself, and gave him a small prick with the needle.

He snorted and jumped a moment, and Cali quickly withdrew and laid flat on the floor as she put the needle in an empty slot in the fabric, rolled it back up, and then stuck it back in her pocket.

Thankfully he didn't wake up, so she carefully made her way back to the door, then back to Estrella when the guard looked back at his phone again.

Slipping out, they carefully closed the door behind them, and joined Peg on the stairs.

"Is he dead?" Peg asked.

"Not yet, but he will be soon. We must leave without being seen."

"Follow me, I know another way out."

By the time they got to the car, Cali was surprised there hadn't been any excitement.

"You sure he's dead?" Estrella asked.

Cali nodded. "The poison I used is lethal."

"What's it do?"

"It causes all your muscles to seize instantly. It lasts for about an hour, or until the muscle dies. The heart, however, is not working during that time, so when it does wear off, the victim is long dead."

"So they don't crap themselves immediately," Estrella said with a nod. "No one will smell it."

"But he will jerk in bed once as his muscles all go stiff, and he then stops snoring. I do not think they will miss that."

"Well, either they missed it, it didn't work, or they're keeping things quiet," Peg said as she pulled out onto the street and headed back to the ranch. "In either case, I'm sure we'll hear all about it in the morning."

A Change of Attitude

"What is so damn important that you needed me to come down here right away this morning!" Sean growled as he stomped into the mayor's office. "A gateway opened just thirty minutes ago, and we've got fighting going on!" He was wearing shorts, a holster, and not much else. He was in his hybrid form as well, and from the number of looks he'd gotten as he'd bulled his way past everyone and up here, no one quite knew what to make of him. The only reason they'd recognized him, he suspected, was because Daelyn, Cali, Peg, and Estrella where with him.

They'd had to drive in, since all the helicopters were in use right now as his troops set up a holding action to let the 70th Armor Regiment get their tanks into action. From the last report he'd gotten, they should be hitting the djevels at the gateway any minute now. Apparently those tanks could go pretty damn fast when they wanted to.

"What are you doing looking like that?" the mayor gasped.

Sean looked around the room. The chief of police was there, as well as the chief of the fire department, the entire city council, and *all* of the other department heads, except Justin apparently. Bill, his father-in-law, was somewhere on the road behind him, and Claudia had already told him she had better things to do today than listen to what she already suspected was coming.

"I was about to put my armor on when you called. I would have come naked, but I figured you wouldn't appreciate that, so I put my shorts back on first."

"I, I meant why aren't you human?"

"Because *this* is the real me." Sean scanned the room again, only this time he growled. "Apparently several of you seem to have gotten the impression that the kind-looking young man who sits here every week and puts up with all your shit is the real me."

There were several gasps at that.

"That kind young man died a long time ago, back when my father was murdered, if you want me to be totally honest. You've all mistaken my patience for naiveté. Well, guess what? That ran out yesterday. Now I've got a war to fight and not a lot of time for petty-ass politics. What is so damned important that you had to have me here?"

"Justin is dead," Sid, the Chief of Police, said.

"Justin?" Sean asked looking confused. Oh, he knew who Justin was, and he had a fairly good idea of what had happened to him, but he wasn't going to give them the satisfaction.

"The man you argued with yesterday."

"I didn't argue with anybody," Sean said. "I just listened to an incredibly rude, self-centered, and conceited man lecture me about things I knew to be complete bullshit."

"You said you were going to kill him!"

"No, I said once martial law was declared I'd execute him for being a traitor. So he's dead? What does that have to do with me?"

"Sean," the mayor said in a placating voice, "after you left, your wife Peg there had some very, well, *nasty*, things to say about Justin. She told us he'd be dead by morning, and he *is*."

"The sun also came up this morning. You blaming them for that as well?" Sean growled.

"Sean! This is serious! Justin was murdered, and one your wives killed him! Peg even told us they would."

"Oh? Was he hacked to death?"

"What? Lord no!"

"Then it wasn't Estrella, cause that's how she kills people. Did he look like a used pincushion? Was he stuck full of knives? No?" Sean asked as the mayor again shook her head.

"Then it wasn't Cali, because that's what she would have done. Me? I'd have ripped off his head or one of his arms. But then I know I didn't do it, because I was spending the night having sex with my wives. Which is how I know they didn't do it either, because they were all there!"

"You can't expect me to believe that, young man!" Sid yelled.

"Oh, shit," Sean heard Bill's voice from the door. Obviously he'd just walked into the room.

Sean had taken a step towards Sid, but he stopped and thought about what he was going to do next. He couldn't beat these people like a bad habit, because frankly he needed them. But, as he'd told the others yesterday, he was taking over.

It was time to lower the boom.

"Okay," Sean said in a soft voice, causing all of them, despite the angry look on his face, to lean in closer so they could hear what he was saying. "This is the way things are going to be from now on. I'm in charge."

"What! No! You can't be serious!" They all started talking at once.

Sean cast a mass silence spell, shutting them up instantly. They looked surprised as their mouths kept moving, but no words came out.

"I am declaring martial law. I am now the military mayor, or governor if you will, of Everything North of Carson City. You can bitch about it all you want, but that's the way it is. Mayor Schiere, you will continue as the acting mayor of Reno until this war is over, because I don't have the time to deal with the day-to-day details. But you will be taking orders from me. All of you will."

Sean noticed someone mouth the words 'I quit', and he smiled, slowly, showing lots of teeth.

"The only way *any* of you get to quit will be because I killed you. Understand? You all went though a lot of hard work to get your jobs, your positions, and you enjoyed them, as well as the benefits that came with them.

"Well, guess what? Playtime is over, and the party has ended. Now you get to *pay* for everything you've done, all you've gained. The only way out now is feet first, and if I think *any* of you are sandbagging me, I'll be the one sending you," Sean lowered his voice into a deep growl then, "*understand*?"

He noticed a lot of shocked looks around the room.

"If you go outside and listen, right now you'll hear a lot of explosions going off in the distance. That's the 70th Armor Regiment, fighting djevels. Every once in a while you might hear a whole bunch go off at once. That's a tank being destroyed, and three people *I* ordered to go out there and die for you ungrateful bastards getting killed. I've been asked repeatedly since I left here yesterday to do my best to defend Reno. So I'm going to do it. And all of *you*," Sean looked around the room again, "are going to do *your* damnedest to help, or you will *die* trying.

"I'm not playing around anymore. You all seem to have forgotten just who and what I am, and while I may not be *your* god, my people are dying out there by the dozens, the hundreds, sometimes even the *thousands*, to save your worthless asses. I owe it to them to come in here and kick your asses into line, so I'm doing it."

Sean turned back to the mayor. "Start evacuating anyone who's willing to go, especially women and children. At least mothers and their children. The fewer people we have to defend, the easier it will be."

Sean waved his hand and dropped the spell. "There's a war on people, now get to work!"

"But, but what about Justin?" someone asked.

"Promote who ever was under him, obviously," Sean said and, turning on his heel, he stalked out of the room, nodding to Bill as he passed him, with Daelyn, Cali, Estrella, and Peg, who was smiling happily, behind him.

"Well," Bill said with a big smile on his face as he clapped his hands. "That went well!"

"That was well?" the mayor asked, eyes wide.

"Lions have nasty tempers. I thought for sure I was going to find half of you dead by the time I got here."

"You're not joking, are you, Bill?" Sid asked.

Bill shook his head. "Not even a little bit. I guess I'm partially to blame. I should have warned you, but then, I honestly didn't think any of you would be as stupid as that Justin guy was. Well, he's dead now and you all better remember that lesson."

"What lesson?"

"That getting in a lion's face is often fatal."

"So Sean did kill him then?"

Bill snorted. "Sean doesn't have the time to sneak into someone's house and kill them. He would have just walked in here, shot him, and left, while you all watched, unable to do a thing to stop him.

"I don't know who killed Justin, and I don't care. You heard the lion. You have a job to do, and your continued survival, as well as that of a couple hundred thousand other people, depends on it.

"Now, let's get to work."

"How long do you think you have until the governor calls you?" Peg asked as they drove back to the ranch.

"I'm more worried about the president," Sean replied.

"Eh, too many cooks," Daelyn said as she sent them sliding around the on ramp, passing all the cars on it in the process in the blink of an eye.

"I must agree," Estrella said. "A divided command never works."

"Plus I'm a lion, right?" Sean said with a chuckle.

"Well, I may be just a tiny bit biased there," Estrella admitted.

"I am surprised you haven't asked us how we did it," Cali said.

Sean leaned back in his seat. "I said you didn't, so obviously you didn't. He must have just fallen down that elevator shaft and landed on all those bullets."

"Huh?" Estrella said with a confused look on her face.

"Modern culture reference," Peg supplied.

"I'll show it to you later, Stell," Cali said with a smile and patted her leg.

"Guess I know what movie we're watchin' tonight," Daelyn chuckled.

"Hopefully I'll be joining you," Sean said, looking out the window.

"What? You got other plans, Lion-boy?"

"Well, there *is* a war on, as I recall."

"Yeah, but you sent those tanks to deal with it. Let 'em have their way with it. They ain't gonna learn if you don't let them fight."

"Still, I need to fly out there and check on things."

"You just don't want to be here if the governor calls!" Peg said with a snicker.

"Okay, okay, I'll come back and watch the movie with you." Sean sighed, but he was smiling. "But I am getting tired of sitting in that office all the time. We've got one more gateway 'til the main event, and I just don't want to miss anything important."

"With all the people you have working for you now, I don't think you have any worries on that score, Love," Estrella told him.

"Then why was I one of the few who went and set up a bunch of safe houses?"

"Well, I don't think most are really going to need them. They're more for the people caught behind the lines, right?"

Sean nodded.

"And anyone caught behind them is either working for us and we sent them there, or somebody who didn't run when we told them too."

"In which case, not our problem," Daelyn agreed.

Sean thought about that. Refugees were definitely going to become a major problem. He just hoped it wasn't one he'd have to deal with. As they pulled into the driveway, a thought occurred to him.

"Dae?"

"Yeah, Sean?"

"Put together a crew and move all our tag and necklace machines into the dwarven halls, please? I don't think it's safe to leave them here anymore."

"All of 'em?"

"I'll talk to Rox and see if she can get Ted to set something up in Vegas. If so, we'll send a set down there."

"Or we could just send half of them to the dwarven hall outside Vegas, ye know."

Sean looked at Daelyn, who was smiling at him smugly as she stopped the car.

Sean leaned over and kissed her. "Thanks for the reminder. Yes, do that."

Getting out of the car, Sean helped the others out. Three in the back was a little tight in the 'Cuda, but the girls didn't seem to mind, and it *was* a lot faster than the van.

Giving each of them a kiss, he then headed to Roxy's office.

"What's up?" she asked as he came in.

"You are. Gear up, you and I are going to go check on the battle, then I think we're going to fly south and look for where we're going to move all of this." He waved his arm around.

Standing up, Roxy nodded. "My gear's with yours. When are you thinking of moving everything?"

"Nonessential stuff can start going as soon as we pick a new place. The rest of it?" Sean gave a small shrug. "We'll pull out when it becomes too risky to stay."

"Not going to put it all in Reno?"

Sean shook his head. "Not anymore. We can stage out of Reno temporarily, but I'm thinking something down around Carson City. Either in town or out by Lyon Peak."

"Don't the dwarves have an exit up there?" she asked as they headed for the armory.

Sean nodded. "I want to be close to them, so if we're taken by surprise, we have someplace safe for our people to retreat to. Plus it'll shorten our supply lines, now that a lot of our parts are coming from them."

"It still seems a bit unreal to be talking about Reno and all the rest falling to the djevels."

"I'm so numb to it, I don't care anymore." Sean sighed. "I remember when we bought this place I thought we'd never have to move again. But here it is not even two years later, and we're doing exactly that."

They stopped by the planning room on the way there so Sean could request his helicopter, then they geared up and went outside. Not surprisingly, Travis was there, along with a half dozen of his security team.

"Sometimes I think you have me bugged," Sean said to Travis as they boarded.

"Huh, hadn't thought about that. Jordan! Make a note; we need to bug Sean in the future."

"You got it, Boss!"

Shaking his head, Sean moved into the copilot's seat across from Trey and put on a headset.

"Where to?" Trey asked.

"I want to check out how the fight's going. After that, fly down to Carson City and check the outskirts."

"What are we looking for?"

"A new base."

We moving?"

"Eventually. Now, let's go."

Sean looked around a lot as they got airborne and headed off to the current battle. Things really hadn't changed all that much from up here, if you discounted the occasional convoy. It wasn't until they got closer to the battle that he saw the scars left by all the previous battles at the previous gateways. There'd been about a hundred of them by now, and there were going to be a couple hundred more before all this was over.

Trey started to fly lower as he got closer, until eventually he was maybe fifty feet above the ground and skirting around the hills instead of flying over them.

"I'm gonna set you down here, Sean. I can't get any closer without coming into their sights."

"Okay. Don't go too far away. We're not going to be here long. Which way is the command post?"

"Due north of us. You can't miss it."

"Thanks!" Sean looked around the back. "Let's go!"

Trey moved off as soon as they were out of the helicopter. Trudging up the side of the small hill, they dropped low and looked over it.

The command post was maybe a hundred yards away, just below the top of another rise. Getting up, they double-timed their way over there, being quickly passed through by the sentries. He found Roloff, the dwarf general Chad had put in charge, up by the crest of the hill, watching the battle below.

"How are we doing, Roloff?" Sean asked.

Roloff looked at him, gave him a nod, then went back to watching the battle.

"Not too bad. Those boys in their armor sure do seem to know their jobs right well. But the devils down there, they're starting to figure out how to deal with 'em. They're pushin' real hard, too. Real hard. About has hard as they did with the last large gate."

"I'm looking for a place down around Carson City to set up for when we get pushed off our hill. Something close to your hall. Any suggestions?"

"Yah. Take over Minden-Tahoe Airport. It's already got everything you need, it's close to town, and we have an old tunnel that runs out by there we can fix up easily enough."

Sean snorted. "I don't know if I can afford to buy an airport."

"I didn't say to buy it, Sean. I said to take it over. You already declared martial law in Reno. Might as well grab that, too."

"How'd you hear about that? I only did it a half hour ago!"

Roloff looked at him and grinned. "What, you don't think I got my own spies in city hall? Plus, Bill called and told me. If yer worried about it, call the governor and tell him you're going to take it. Not everyone is ignoring the coming battle. Besides, if you call the governor and talk to him, he'll feel like he's still got some say in what's going on."

"Ugh, politics."

"It's the ugly part of the war, don't I know!"

Sean had to agree with that. He spent another few minutes watching the battle and listening to Roloff as he directed the fight. They'd only lost three tanks so far, but the fight was still young. But he saw enough to know tank combat wasn't something he knew anything about. Grabbing Roxy and the others, he called Trey back and went to the pick up point.

"Where to?" Trey asked.

"Minden Airport." Sean cast a silence spell on the helicopter and looked around at the others. "Anybody got a cellphone I can borrow?"

"I do," Roxy said. "Who do you need to call?"

"The governor. I figure he'd probably like to hear what I've been doing."

"Ya' think?" Roxy said with a laugh. "Just a minute and I'll get him on the phone for you."

§

Sean padded over to where the First was holding court and flopped down onto the ground nearby.

"Rough day?"

"Yeah, I had to pretend to be you." Sean sighed as the others chuckled.

The First laughed. "I heard. Estrella was quite impressed with you reading them the riot act and putting your foot down."

"Oh yeah, I put it down alright. On their necks," Sean said with a snort.

"You gave them every chance, Son. Honestly, I think you gave them too many, but you're still learning."

"I know, I know. I'm going around in either my hybrid or full lion form from now on. I don't think I'll be doing 'human Sean' for a long, long time."

"They do need a constant reminder. Still, I'm sure they'll get over it."

"They'll never look at me the same again. I killed one of their friends, then I rubbed their noses in it. People don't care much for that, Dad."

"You didn't kill him, one of your wives did," the First pointed out.

Sean laughed. "Yeah, like they're going to make that distinction. Then I had to talk to the governor and tell him I was taking over Reno, and 'oh, if you don't mind, I'm taking over an airport, too.'"

"I'm surprised you bothered to call him," Keairra said.

"Like it or not, I still need his help. I don't *want* to run everything myself. I just want them to do what I tell them to and not play stupid games."

"What's the airport for?" the First asked.

"We need someplace to go when we get pushed off our hill. Originally I thought we'd use Reno, but Chad is pretty certain we won't be able to hold it."

"Raban is holding Munich."

"Raban is fighting what? Hundreds? Maybe a thousand? You heard what Estrella saw. We're going to be fighting *millions*. We've got lords and their magic users, and who knows? A prince or two may decide to join the fight."

"So what *did* the governor say?" Keairra asked.

"He understood what I was doing, even if he wasn't happy about it. He even believed me when I told him I had no idea who killed that asshole or why, but that I was going to milk it for all it was worth to get everyone off their asses and working on survival."

"Well, it's a start at least."

"Yeah, it's a start, but it's probably too little, too late. We've got, what? Six days until the main gateway opens? I'm still pushing for more artillery pieces, more soldiers, more bullets, more rifles, more bombs, more of everything. There's always some asshole somewhere who decides we don't need what we asked for, screwing everything up and causing a shortage or a delay."

Sean shook his head. "There are times when I'm tempted to call up Cali's relatives and have them kill a whole bunch of worthless paper-pushers."

"Well, maybe you should," the First said with a serious look.

"You can't be serious," Sean said with a groan.

"Son, I hate to do this to you, but you're going to have to do some very nasty things here in the next few years. The kinds of things I'm sure you're going to have a long time reconciling with your conscience."

Sean sighed heavily, dropping his head. "Now what?"

"You're going to have to cut off their food supply."

"Isn't that the whole reason we're doing this?" Sean grumbled.

"I don't mean like that. I mean if they take a town and it's full of people. You're going to have to kill *all* those people before the demons can eat them."

Sean blinked. "Wait, what?"

"You'll have to kill them. When you pull out of Reno, you're either going to have to nuke it, or build one of your bombs and set it off."

"I can't do that!"

"Sorry, you can, and you will."

"But I'll be murdering thousands! Tens of thousands! Maybe more!"

The First walked over to him and placed a paw on his shoulders. "What do the demons do to humans?"

"They eat them. But that doesn't mean we should just kill them all; we might save a few!"

"No, Son," the First said, shaking his head, "they don't eat them, they eat their *souls*. They destroy everything there is. They take away the afterlife; they take away whatever it is that humans fundamentally are; they take away their chance at going on to the next stage in their existence.

"What they do is far worse than killing them. You're doing them a huge favor by killing any human before they can be eaten. Remember, they're all going to die one day. But if they die by your hand, at least their soul moves on."

"You're a bastard, you know that?" Sean growled. "And just how am I to explain that away when I do it?"

"Lying works," Keairra said with a shrug.

"Also, if you wait until the city or town has been overrun, you can claim you were attacking the demons," the First said, continuing. "No one is going to know there were any humans left alive unless you tell them. You can claim they were all dead, you can claim you got them out. I'll tell you right now, your president, your senior military leaders? They're all going to understand *exactly* what you did, because I'm going to have Tisha remind them.

"But I'm sorry, this isn't going to win you any popularity contests. Once we've won, everyone will be happy. They'll get over it."

"Yeah, right," Sean said, sighing as he rolled over onto his back. "It's been seventy years since World War Two ended, and people are still going after the people who won it for the way they did it."

"Seventy years from now, you may be living here with the rest of us waiting for your turn in the queue," Keairra pointed out.

"Maybe sooner than that if I lose this war," Sean grumbled. "Having to be so positive all the time, so gung-ho, so certain, and doing everything I can to inspire the others, that really wears me down. I have no idea how you all make it look so easy."

Keairra laughed. "Adam says the same thing about you, you know. He wants to know how you make it all look so easy, and at your age, too! You've actually made him *jealous*."

"Adam? Jealous of me?" Sean shook his head thinking about that.

"It's the best thing that's happened to him in a very long time. He's finally trying to do all those things his father and I tried for centuries to get him to do. We're very happy someone finally got through to him."

"Huh, what did that?"

Keairra gave him a very toothy grin. "They told him, in graphic detail no less, about all those people you killed and how you did it. Adam thought *he* had a temper! Learning you have one that trumps his was quite a shock."

"Learning they all love you for it was an even bigger one," Sampson said, coming over from the edge of the group. Sean hadn't even noticed him lying over there.

Rolling to his feet, Sean shifted into his hybrid form and gave Sampson a hug.

"Look, Sean. I know it's tough going, but the First is right. These are things that have to be done, and sadly, it's going to be up to you to do them. It's your duty, whether you like it or not."

"I know, I know. It's just, this is the only place I can actually bitch about it," Sean said with a wry grin.

"How's your mother doing?"

"Quite well, actually. For a while, I think she was seeing Arthur over at Sapientia, but I don't think she is anymore. She's stopped hiding her age."

"Her age?"

"She's part faerie, so she was hiding the fact that she looks a lot younger than she actually is…and well, Arthur is old, and he looks it."

"Well, maybe when this is all over, she can return to Ireland to look for someone new," Sampson said a little heavily. "After all, I think she'll admit that you don't need watching over anymore."

"I have kids now, Sampson. She's got grandkids. I don't think she's going to move *that* far away.

"That reminds me. I'm supposed to be watching a movie with the wives and the kids. I'm honestly surprised they haven't woken me up yet."

"Well, say hi to your mother and everyone else for me."

"What, not Roberta?" Sean teased.

"She's your wife now, Sean. I don't think you'd appreciate me talking with her, even from the grave," Sampson said with a small smile.

Sean nodded. If Sampson were to suddenly come back to life, he'd be pretty antsy about it if he came around Roberta, even though he still saw him as a father figure.

Closing his eyes, Sean woke himself up on the couch.

"Have a nice nap?" Jolene asked, leaning against him.

Sean nodded and noticed that the movie was almost done.

"Good, because have we got plans for *you.*"

Boss Meetings

"Steven! I'm so glad to see you're okay!" the president said, shaking hands with him. "And Tisha, it's always a pleasure to see you." He turned and shook hands with her next.

"I thought it wasn't a big deal for a lycan to get shot?" said Linda Welsh, the newly appointed CIA director.

"Yeah, that's what I thought, right up until I got shot," Steve said with a shake of his head. "It might not kill you, but *damn* did it hurt!"

"At least you're protected from silver now," Director Kensington of the Secret Service said.

"I'd heard they used silver bullets," the president said, waving them over to a couple of seats. "Sit! Take a load off. How's your man doing?"

"Oh, he's fine," Steve said, sitting down by Carl Mince, who was the Secret Service's head of their new lycan division. "But I've been warning everyone for a while now that sooner or later, these ALS people would try to kill me again."

The president nodded. "I had a talk with the Department of Justice. I've asked them to look into using the RICO Act to put an end to these people."

The head of Homeland Security spoke up as well. "I've also directed the FBI to start a full investigation of this 'Anti-Lycan Society'. The two truck bombs the police found with those fanatics in Reno? There's no way they could have gotten those on their own, and we know they worked with the ALS in the past, especially since it was ALS lawyers who got their people out of jail."

Steve smiled. "Thank you for that, I'll be sure to let Sean know. We had no idea where those bombs came from, and I know they've been very worried about a repeat."

"Yes, well, unfortunately the agent in charge of the group that discovered the whole plot sat on the original reports. He tried to fire the two who leaked them to your governor."

"He did?"

"Don't worry," Kensington said, smiling, "they work for me now. With the things they're able to do with statistics, I figure we're going to need them after those gateways go away."

"So, Steven," the president said. "What does bring you here today?"

"Well, the first was those ALS idiots; we came to file a formal complaint with the government and ask for your help in putting an end to them. As that appears to be well in hand now, there's a special request from Sean."

"Oh? What does he want?"

"Tactical nuclear warheads," Steve said with a serious expression.

Everyone looked at each other, then back at Steve.

"Why?" the president asked.

"Because there are times ahead when he's going to need to deny those demons certain 'things'…"

"Like food," Tisha said, interrupting them. "He's going to have to destroy any large concentrations of food they gather to keep them from gaining strength and reproducing."

"Food?" Carl said, looking around, "but I thought they ate…"

"People," Steve said with a heavy sigh that wasn't at all faked.

"People's *souls*, to be specific," Tisha added. "Understand, if a devil eats your soul, that's it. You don't go to the afterlife or whatever it is you humans move on to after you die."

"So it's not *just* a matter of denying them food, it's also a matter of saving souls. *Human* souls."

Steve and Tisha watched as they all digested that.

"What about your 'godly wrath'?" Kensington asked after a few moments.

"Using that is a bit involved," Tisha said. "It's also something the djevels aren't familiar with, so we're saving it for specific acts."

"You know I can't just hand over nuclear weapons," the president said.

"We know," Steve replied, nodding. "That's why Sean asked me to bring it up now, before they're needed. So you can figure out what needs to be done. Sean doesn't actually need them *personally*. But a military group under his command? They could control and set off any devices that were used. This would allow you to still control them via those failsafe codes you use."

"Please understand, we want those devices to *require* those codes to be used," Tisha said, "so if the unthinkable happens and one ends up in the wrong hands, they can't set it off."

"So you're saying we'd still have final approval before any weapon was detonated?" General Baker asked, speaking up for the first time.

"Yes," Steve and Tisha both said at the same time.

"Mr. President, we have groups that are approved to handle and deploy with warheads. As long as we don't give them the codes to detonate the bombs, they can't be used."

"So you're saying we should do this, General?" the president asked.

"I'm saying we *can* do this. The procedures and practices already exist. Whether or not we do this, well, that's up to you, Sir, not me. I will, however, start an immediate review of our practices and procedures, so if you should order it, we'll be ready."

"Thank you, General." The president turned back to Steve and Tisha. "I'll have to talk with my full cabinet as well as the congressional leaders. I'll admit to having some reservations, mainly because I'm no expert on nuclear weapons."

Steve nodded. "I don't think we can ask for anything more, Sir." Steve paused a moment, and then smiled. "Well, actually, there is one more thing I'd like to ask for your permission on."

"And that would be?"

"I'd like to take my recruitment team to Walter Reed."

"Why would you want to go there?" General Baker asked, sitting up straight very quickly.

"Well, simply put, I found out recently that under certain circumstances, we can help some of the more severely wounded."

"What?"

"It's like this," Tisha said. "When you're infected, if you have a fresh wound, it will heal back to normal."

"What do you mean by 'fresh'?"

"If you cut off the stump of a man who lost his leg, the whole leg will grow back. But only if you infect them then and there."

General Baker moved back an inch in his chair, blinking. "You can do that?"

"Not always, and there *are* risks involved," Steve said. "But with your permission, we'd like to start going through those who were wounded in the last war and heal those we can, assuming, of course, they wish to become lycans."

"If you can heal those men, you not only have my permission," the president said, "you have my blessings."

"Mine, too," General Baker said. "I'll have my office contact you as soon as I get back to the Pentagon to arrange the details."

"Well, unless there's something else?" the president asked, looking around as everyone shook their heads.

"Then I guess this meeting is adjourned."

Getting up, Steve and Tisha left the oval office, heading back to their car.

"Just a moment, if you please?" Carl asked, trotting over to them.

"Sure, Carl," Steve said as he walked along with them. "What's up?"

"I heard a rumor that some guy in Reno got whacked last night? Some sort of minor government flunky who pissed Sean off?"

Steve shrugged. "I haven't heard anything about it. If Sean had done it, trust me, he would have called and warned me about it. Tish?"

Tisha shook her head. "I know he's starting to crack the whip; the main gateway opens soon, and he's trying to get as many evacuated as he can. But he hasn't killed anybody yet."

"I like how you qualify things," Carl said with a sigh.

Tisha shrugged, grinning. "We're lions, not saints, Carl."

"Well, thanks for letting me know."

"Anytime, Carl," Steve said as he and Tisha waved and continued on to their car.

"Is this anything I should know about?" Steve asked Tisha in a soft voice.

"All I know is Sean didn't do it, doesn't know who did, and doesn't care."

"Well, that's good enough for me, I guess."

Ξ

King Sladd strode into his throne room, his princes arrayed before him, prostrating themselves to him, as always.

"Arise!" he commanded and watched as they all stood before him. Their entourages were the smallest he'd seen in a long time, the majority of their lieutenants being involved in overseeing the preparations in their masters' absence. Also the little execution the last time he'd summoned them all was probably still fresh in their minds. So anyone they valued was also left behind today.

The master gateway would open a day's ride from King Sladd's castle. While custom and the law forbade the killing of lords, princes, and most especially kings during a pass, if you killed the king and took his place, there would be no one left to punish you for your transgression.

Knowing this, King Sladd had moved his castle away from the hellige for the master gateway, where the armies were gathering for their upcoming attacks. He had himself killed the previous king of this area halfway through a pass, when the king's armies were in the field and his defenses were thin, overly relying on laws and customs. Quite foolishly, in Sladd's opinion.

Thankfully, none of the current princes were alive back then; King Sladd had been rather quick to scour them from his new court. But he wouldn't put it past some of the other kings, and especially not past Queen Dragkedja, to educate his current set in the hopes of sowing discord she could put to her own advantage once the permanent gate opened.

There were no dedicated hellige points for a permanent gate. It could form literally anywhere, though normally it was drawn to the nearest point, if one were close enough. He had his seers and his scholars researching the process; it had been a very long time since the last one, after all, and sadly his kind were not known for their meticulousness when it came to record keeping.

"Report on your readiness," King Sladd said and pointed towards Prince Talt, who spent the next hour defining succinctly everything he had been doing and was preparing to do.

For the next six hours, King Sladd listened to their reports. Princes Lykta and Vises Ikke were the only two with something different to report from the others. They had split their forces into four groups each and deployed them across King Sladd's domain so they could quickly respond to the lille helliges wherever they should open up.

"Princes Lykta and Vises Ikke, I am pleased with your insight and resourcefulness in dealing with the task I have set upon you. If you should continue with such diligence, I suspect I will be forced to reward you," King Sladd said with a smile.

The two princes smiled back, looking pleased with themselves.

The expressions on the other four, especially Prince Talt, were much more guarded. King Sladd laughed to himself; if nothing else, a little infighting and oneupmanship would help keep Prince Talt at bay for a while.

"The master gateway will open soon; you are all dismissed," King Sladd said with a wave of his hand and watched as they carefully withdrew. After they had gone, his chief advisor entered the room and bowed low before the throne.

"King Sladd, I would speak."

King Sladd nodded. "What is it, Eldstaden?"

"Our records on the locations for the permanent gateway and much of the lore that surrounds such a thing is lacking, as I am sure you are already aware?"

King Sladd nodded.

"It has been noted that there is one, however, who would know all about it."

"You are talking about the master of the ley-lines who lives upon the mountain of the dead, are you not?"

Eldstaden nodded. "Yes, Your Majesty. It occurs to me and others that perhaps we should go ask him about this."

"The mountain of the dead lies well outside of my domain, Eldstaden. I have no power there. Further, the lore tells us he is surrounded by many defenses that are deadly to our kind."

"True, Your Majesty. The lore does tell us that. But we've recently come to realize that much of our lore is based on things with no written records or recorded history. So is it true? Or is it just the excuses of failure by those who were not up to the task? Our lore also tells us we took this world by gaining mastery over all those who had gone before, does it not?"

King Sladd nodded, conceding the point.

"Then perhaps it is time we send some new people to the mountain to see if the master of the ley-lines is still protected, and if he is not, to see if he can answer our questions."

King Sladd thought about that; it was a good question, and it was true that for as long as he could remember, no one had ventured there.

"You raise interesting ideas, Eldstaden. Do you have a group in mind for this adventure?"

"Several actually, Your Highness. If nothing else, they will let us gauge the strength and effectiveness of the defenses."

"And if they should prove to still be all they are rumored to be?"

Eldstaden smiled a smile of pure evil. "Why then, Your Majesty, you command Prince Talt to deal with the problem."

King Sladd laughed loudly for several minutes at the blunt boldness of his advisor's command.

"As always, Eldstaden, you never fail to bring me the most enjoyable solutions to my current problems. Send those you have chosen for the task and entertain me with the results. And perhaps we shall challenge our most dangerous prince with this task, should they fail to return."

Storm Watch

"So that's it," Sean said, looking at the gateway through a set of binoculars.

"I guess so," Chad said. "You know, for some reason, I thought it would look different."

Sean nodded. "Me, too. I have to give Deidre credit; it opened pretty close to where she predicted it would." Sean lowered the binoculars again and looked at all the activity going on around and behind him. An engineering division of sappers was hard at work setting up fortifications and emplacements while the rest of the army dug in. Surprisingly, a large number of the engineers were badger lycans, something he hadn't run into before he'd met them. Looking them over, he thought he'd like tangling with them even less than with a boar.

"When are you going to start shelling them?" Sean asked.

"Any moment. I just gave the order now that we no longer have any aircraft in the area."

Sean heard it then, the whistling of air, and apparently the djevels heard it too, because they started working a lot more frantically as the first shell landed, quickly followed by four more.

"How long are you going to keep it up for?" Sean asked.

"As long as I can. Then we've got an aerial bombardment planned. I want to give our people all the time I can to get set up for the fight."

Sean nodded and went back to watching the enemy. The evacuation of the local area hadn't gone as quickly as he would have liked; he'd had to order his men to resort to force. The words of the First about denying the enemy food were still in his ears, and the last thing he wanted to do was to start killing people.

He wanted it to literally be the last thing he did, because he didn't doubt the time would come when he'd have to start doing it.

The evacuation of Reno was also going slower than expected. People had gotten used to the sounds of combat off in the hills every two or three days, so when the order to evacuate had come down, a lot of them just ignored it. After all, they hadn't been bothered yet, so why should they be in the future?

"I heard a small town got wiped out last night up around Paradise Valley?" Chad asked as he alternated between reading reports on his laptop and watching what was going on around him.

"Yeah, seems some djevels got away from us last week. By the time our hunters and trackers caught up with them, it was too late. Apparently all the fighting made more than a few people think it was some sort of Fourth of July display, and they wandered right into the middle of it and were killed," Sean said, shaking his head.

"That sucks. What were they doing that far north? Don't they usually head south towards Reno, or west towards Tahoe?"

"Either they got lost, or they were just a little smarter than the rest." Sean watched as a shell landed in one of the ditches the djevels were digging, causing a black mist of vaporized djevel parts. "How long do you think until they get that thing built?"

Chad shook his head. "If they showed us everything they had last time, it'll be weeks, maybe months. My problem is, I can't keep shelling them forever. Our stock of shells are limited, the guns wear out, and replacement parts are also limited. I'm going to take random breaks after the second day and throw air strikes at them, tank attacks, infantry, you name it."

"Can't the dwarves keep you supplied?"

"We're already stretching their capacity with armor, firearms, and bullets. They're also giving us shells for the tanks, which are incredibly useful, but from what the supply people are telling me, the government used up a lot of our stockpiles in the Middle East over the last few decades, and they weren't terribly interested in replacing them because of budget issues."

"Great, just great."

"Hey, look on the bright side."

"There's a bright side?"

"Originally we were planning on fighting this with swords and shields. Now we've got automatic weapons, bombs, artillery, mines, all sorts of toys!" Chad said with a smile.

"Just a moment ago you were making it sound all doom and gloom."

"Well, it's not going to be *easy*; we know they've got millions, and anyone we kill comes back in a week. We're gonna suffer setbacks, and I don't think we're going to stop them getting their bridgehead built. Those are just the facts of life, and we all need to accept it.

"Remember, the goal is to keep the permanent gate from forming. Nothing else matters until we've achieved that."

"And that's a year away." Sean sighed. "Look, I'm gonna have a box shipped out here. It's going to be a mine, a really big mine, and I'm gonna be the only one who can set it off. Don't even try to open it."

"Doomsday weapon?"

"Yeah, it'll probably kill everything within a half mile instantly. So we're not gonna use it until everyone has been pushed back."

"You know it won't stop them, right?"

Sean nodded. "I'm not planning on using it until the time is right. So make sure those engineers do a good job of hiding it so the djevels don't find it. And remember, it's booby-trapped. So don't even try to open it."

"Got it. Anything else?"

"I don't even know where to start anymore. Between the city council, the mayor, the governor, the military, the magic uses, lycans, and the president, these last few days have been a stone cold bitch."

"Well, at least you put the fear of god in 'em, right?" Chad asked with a grin.

"I put the fear of something in them—well, some of them at least. I'm going back to the ranch; let me know if anything changes. I have a lot of people wanting answers to questions, and I don't know what to tell them."

"I hate defensive actions. There's no real winning them in the long run; the enemy always holds the best cards, and you don't get to see them until it's too late and he plays his hand. We're in react mode, and that always puts us behind the power curve."

"I know, I know," Sean admitted. "I'll see you at tonight's staff meeting."

Chad nodded, and Sean made the trek back to the landing zone for the helicopters, Travis and the rest of his bodyguards forming up in a lose circle around him. That was another thing he hated: since the main gateway was now open, he had bodyguards twenty-four seven. About the only time he was left alone was when he was in the bedroom with his wives.

At least they let him have some privacy for those times he was with one of the girls and they *weren't* in the bedroom.

But he couldn't complain; once the djevels got their bridgehead, Chad, Maitland, and he had agreed they'd eventually start sending out teams to find him and kill him because he was the one in charge.

And that reminded him once again of the First's idea for doing the very same thing to the djevels, an idea that had been mentioned how long ago? Sean shook his head and couldn't remember. But the idea had merit, and he knew Chad was just chomping at the bit to do something, *anything*, to the djevels in their homeland.

Perhaps it was something he should bring up at tonight's briefing.

There were other things he needed to attend to as well, now that the skirmishes were over, and the war had begun.

Once they landed, he struck off for the main house in search of his Uncle Philo. It took him a while to find him, and when he did, he was surprised to find him working in the small hospital that Gloria and one of the healers the dwarves had loaned them ran.

"Philo!"

"Yes, Sean?"

"I was wondering, I need a bit of a favor."

"Of course, anything to help out. What is it?"

"Umm," Sean smiled, a little embarrassed. "I need to talk to Markey, your friend. I haven't seen him around here much of late." Sean sighed then.

"Not that I can say I blame him. Hasn't been a lot of fun here lately."

Philo nodded and laughed. "No, it hasn't been the kind of place he prefers to frequent, however, Reno is still full of many of those, and with all the troops here looking for a good time, I do believe he's been enjoying himself."

Sean nodded. "And that's what I wanted to talk to him about."

Philo looked a little shocked. "You don't think he's been taking advantage of them, I hope?"

Sean shook his head. "Quite the opposite. I'm looking to take advantage of *him*."

"How so?"

"Markey's a spirit of mischief, and I've noticed that he's a good soul."

"Of course he is."

"Well, with the war and all that, I'm worried about our people. Any breaks they get are going to be short ones, and I suspect a lot of them are going to be needing whatever fun and relief they can find."

"And?"

"And I wanted to see if Markey would be interested in helping with that. I mean, he's here, so why not see if I can get his help? These next few years are going to be rough, and anything I can do to make it easier on folks, even if it's only for an hour or two, is worth doing."

Philo nodded and after a moment, he smiled. "I see your point, and I think Markey will see it, too. The fact that he's decided to stay here with me rather than return home is something I've found quite curious. I've suspected of late that he's got an interest in the very thing you're suggesting."

"Thanks, Philo. I appreciate it."

"Anytime, Sean. I'll let you know what he decides, if he doesn't tell you himself."

Sean's next stop was to check in with Roxy and Oak on the construction he'd ordered down at Minden Airport to the south of Carson City. It might be months before they had to pull out of here, but there was no reason to wait until the last minute to start.

Sean found Roxy in her office, bent over her desk going over a large set of plans spread over her desk.

"Hi, Hon," she mumbled as Sean came in.

Sean smiled and looked at that nice tight ass of hers; she was swaying back and forth a little bit and humming some tune.

Walking up, he pressed into her from behind, bending over her back to look at what she was doing. Resting his chin on her shoulder, he felt himself growing excited; she'd gone from swaying to slowly grinding back into his crotch.

"What are you looking at?" he asked, wrapping his left arm around her body just below her breasts as his right hand pressed into her hip lightly, then slowly slid down her side, moving under the waistband of her shorts and then her panties.

"I was looking at the site plan for Minden," she said with a husky purr.

"Was?" Sean teased as he pushed her shorts and panties down, his fingers moving around to tease between her legs.

Roxy sighed and spread her legs wider, giving his fingers better access to her sex as she braced her hands on the table, Sean leaning into her a bit more.

"Somebody seems to have different ideas…"

Sean laughed. "Oh, no, please tell me what I'm looking at."

Taking a deep breath, Roxy looked down at the plans below her. "Dae's uncle sent over the site plans. All the stuff printed on it is what's there, the pencil…

Roxy gasped as Sean slid a thick finger up inside her.

Grinning, Sean gave her ear a light nip. "You were saying?"

Roxy squirmed a little back against him and his teasing finger.

"The pencil marks are where…"

Sean added a second finger and rubbed the remaining two over her clit, causing her to get distracted again.

"Bastard," Roxy growled playfully.

"Where…?" Sean teased again.

"Where your dick goes into me and nails my ass to the floor every night!" she growled.

Letting go of her for a moment with his left, Sean grabbed his pants waistband and pushed them down past his hips. While he had the collar now and didn't have to worry about ruining his clothes, he still wore pants with an elastic waistband most of the time, and no belt. He'd gotten to like the looser clothing most lycans wore.

Roxy immediately reached back between her legs and stroked his shaft with her hand.

"Somebody want something?" Sean whispered in her ear.

"Somebody always wants something, and right now, that something is you!"

Putting his left hand on the table to steady himself, Sean withdrew his fingers and moved in closer as Roxy guided him inside her, his fingers stroking slowly over her sex as he slid into familiar depths. No matter how many times he took his Roxy, it was always exciting for him. To take her and reclaim her, again and again.

Roxy's head came down onto the desk, turned to the left as Sean's weight pressed into her body, her eyes focusing on the strong hand there as Sean's hips moved back and forth, sliding that wonderful tool of his in and out of her body.

"Hey, Rox, I…"

Sean looked up; Jolene was standing in the doorway.

"Ah! Get naked and get over here, Jo!" Sean growled and gave Roxy's ear a lick, causing her to shiver.

Jo laughed and came around behind them, trailing pieces of clothing behind her.

"Like I have to be asked. I could use a little recharging!"

Sean moved his right hand up Roxy's body to pinch and pull at her nipples as Jolene put her hands on his body and sank down to her knees, then she turned around and moved into the space beneath them, and put her talented tongue and fingers to use on the two of them.

Sean and Roxy both gave loud sighs of pleasure. Sean noticed that Jolene was using her mind magic; apparently she'd been doing something magical this morning and was tapping the two of them for mana. He'd have to ask later what she'd been up to; his guess was she'd come here for a little recharging, and he'd been lucky enough to be here when she did.

Sean picked up speed then, as Roxy's movements beneath him became more demanding. She was making little growls of pleasure in time to both his thrusts and Jolene's licks. Panting himself, Sean just drove faster and faster, letting Jolene's fingers and tongue carry him along as Roxy twisted and pushed back against him, squeezing tighter and tighter until suddenly they were both there.

Sean held Roxy tight as he emptied himself inside her, Roxy moaning and pressing back against him, keeping him deep inside, while Jolene lovingly teased them both.

When Sean and Roxy had finally settled down, Jolene stroked his balls.

"My turn!" she whispered.

"Oh, I like the sound of that!" Sean said with a grin.

"Ugh, I think I drooled all over the plans," Roxy grumbled.

"Blame it on Sean." Jolene chuckled as Sean slowly withdrew.

"Then they'll all know what we were doing…"

"They already know!"

"I'd rather they just suspected," Roxy growled.

Snickering, Sean picked up Jolene and put her on her back next to Roxy as he moved between Jolene's legs. Bending over, he gave Roxy a kiss as she pushed her body up off of the desk. Then he turned and smiled at Jolene and kissed her.

"Oh! Break time!" Daelyn crowed from the doorway.

"Get naked, you're next," Sean growled as he wondered who else would be wandering in…

Big Time

Sean was sitting at his desk with Cali in his lap, his fingers making inroads on removing her top, when someone tapped on the door.

"Sean?" Peg's voice asked.

"Not a good time," Sean growled, and Cali frowned.

"I know, but you've got a visitor, so if you haven't gotten too carried away?"

Sean sighed and removed his hands from underneath Cali's top, which she then straightened while climbing out of his lap.

"Send them in," Sean grumbled as Cali leaned over to give him a kiss before moving to stand behind his chair.

The door opened then, and Sean saw someone he hadn't seen in well over a year.

"Vincent?" he said, standing up as Vincent Powers, the Sapientia council head for Los Angeles, was shown in by Peg.

"Sean! Cali!" Vincent said with a smile. "Sorry to interrupt," he said, winking at Cali, who grinned back at him. "Nice to see you both again."

Sean reached across the table and shook hands with Vincent when he reached the desk.

"Have a seat," Sean said, motioning towards one of the chairs. "What brings you to Reno?"

"Well," Vincent said taking the offered seat, "Arthur Troy told us you'd asked for a liaison between the magic users and your forces, someone to sit in on your meetings, someone with enough power with the councils to guarantee anything we agreed to."

"And they picked you?" Sean sat down, a bit surprised by that.

"Actually, I volunteered," Vincent said with a smile.

"Really?"

"Well, you did me a big favor when you protected us against that attack, allies or not. Plus I have a lot of pull in Sapientia, and even the Ascendance listen to me now when I talk. So I figured, why not? I think you'll agree, this isn't the time for half measures, am I right?"

Sean laughed. "No, you're right. I'm happy to have you, to be honest. I've been a little worried about who they'd send us. Now that the war has truly begun, I expect things to get hectic and confusing, and even a little desperate at times.

"We don't just need the help of the magic users, we also need to make sure the ones working with us are protected and kept safe. You're going to be one of our most valuable resources, and you're limited, very limited. We can't afford to lose a single one."

Vincent nodded. "Arthur conveyed your concerns to the rest of the councils when this was being discussed. Everyone has come to realize that the lions, and especially you, are men of your word." Vincent grinned then. "They've also realized you're a lot better at kicking ass and taking names then we ever were."

"My husband is a winner," Cali said with a smirk, "and everyone loves a winner."

"All too true, Cali dear. All too true. They sent me up here with a small staff, so I was hoping you could find us a place to stay here with everyone else?"

"It won't be anything like you're used to," Peg warned from the doorway where she was still standing, watching the conversation.

Vincent laughed. "After forty years of living in LA, *nothing* can be like what I'm used to. But don't worry, we'll survive."

Smiling, Sean stood back up. "Well, let's get you settled then. You can introduce me to your team, and I'll introduce you to who you need to know."

"Oh, you don't have to do that. I already feel bad for interrupting."

Sean shook his head, still smiling. "The next meeting is less than an hour away. I'm sure we can pick up where we left off afterwards," Sean said as he turned and smiled at Cali.

The daily briefing started almost on time. Chad was a little late, and they definitely needed to wait for him.

The first thing Sean did was introduce Vincent, noticing there were more than a few pleased looks on the faces of the others. Interacting with the different magic user councils had become something of an issue for several of the people here lately because there was no central point of contact. Vincent would have his work cut out for him, but at least they now had someone to do the work.

"So, Chad," Sean said, starting things off, "how goes our first week?"

"One down, one hundred and three to go. Right now they're still trying to build their fort. I haven't seen any magic users joining the fight, and that worries me."

"Why?" Adam asked.

"This is it; this is what everyone has been waiting for. So why hold back? Why not just go full out, balls to the wall, and send everything?"

"Maybe they're waiting for the portal to grow to a specific size?" Jack suggested.

"Maybe they're hoping to lull us into a false sense of security before they change their tactics in the hope of catching us off guard," Maitland suggested.

"Maybe it's politics," Estrella said.

"How so?" Chad asked as everyone turned to look at her.

"Everyone you kill is going to be out of it for a week. Whoever's leading this attack, they're going to be sent to the back of the line after they've sent everything they have at you. So why waste their best? They're not going to get anything for it, and they know it."

Chad nodded slowly. "I remember you telling me Sladd has six princes, and they'll be what he sends up against us first. Do you think any of the princes will come through?"

"Not unless they're sure of a win. If they get killed, their people won't have a leader for almost a week, and the others will prey on their people."

"I thought there was a rule about no infighting during a pass?" Sean asked.

Estrella snorted. "Only if you get caught. Trust isn't something you want to give a demon…"

"Djevel," Cali interjected with a grin.

Estrella grinned back. "Djevel, excuse me. But they only keep their word and follow the rules when it suits them, or when there's someone bigger and badder enforcing it. These are princes; only the king has that kind of power, and he can't be everywhere."

"Too bad we don't have any spies embedded in their forces." Chad sighed.

Sean agreed. "Yes, but it is what it is, and we have to deal with it."

"Maybe we can interrogate one?" Cali suggested.

"You mean torture, right?" Estrella said. "'Cause that's about the only thing that'll get one to talk."

Cali grinned. "Of course!"

"They can be tortured?" Chad said, looking surprised.

Estrella nodded, and Cali shrugged.

"No harm in trying, right?" Cali said.

"You two figure something out," Sean said. "Now, let's get back on track."

Chad went back to talking about what they'd used in resources so far today, then engaged the logistics people, Majors Randy Harper and Joyce Vanderberg, as well as Jack, Maitland, Roloff, and even Vincent, as he discussed supply issues and troop on- and off-duty schedules.

Sean listened carefully and was thinking about the first week's fighting, all the munitions that had been consumed, as Chad went over the current numbers and his projections. Yeah, they'd killed hundreds, probably thousands. But a week from now they'd all be back. The weapons, however, would not. Only if a lion killed them would they not reincarnate.

If only there was a weapon…

If only…

Suddenly it hit him.

"FUCK!" Sean said, jumping to his feet and looking around the table. "We gotta go back!"

Everyone froze and stared at him.

"What?" Roxy asked after a moment.

"We gotta go back! Fuck fuck fuck! I can't believe I missed it!" Sean said as he started to pace back and forth, his tail lashing behind him. "How the *hell* did that happen!"

"What are you talking about? Go back where?"

"To the Onderwereld! Damn, I'm gonna have to talk to the First about this. Chad, you're going to have to work out a strategy for me to lead a team in there. We can use one of the small gates," Sean said as he started to think about what it would take, still pacing, eyes down in thought.

"Whoa! Slow down there just a minute, Sean!" Roxy growled, and everyone was staring at him now like he'd lost all sense.

"It's obvious! And I *completely* missed it!" Sean growled loudly.

"Yeah, well, maybe you'll share with the rest of us then, Lion-boy? 'Cause we got no idea what in the hell you're talking about," Daelyn grumbled and smacked him on the ass, *hard.*

Sean laughed and dropped back into his seat, taking a moment to kiss Daelyn and then Roxy.

"Okay, some of you know we found an alien living in the Onderwereld. His people are the ones who accidentally let the djevels in countless millennia ago. Remember?"

Sean noticed a few of the heads around the table were nodding, cautiously. The rest were looking surprised by the little piece of knowledge Sean had been careful *not* to share before now.

"Well, he *told* us—Estrella and me, that is—that they had a big war with the djevels and killed all of them. But they missed a few who reproduced out of sight, and when they came back in greater numbers than before, Mahkiyoc said they'd let the weapons fall into disrepair and they weren't able to fix them in time."

Sean noticed that Maitland suddenly facepalmed, and Chad was starting to look embarrassed.

"Yeah, they were stupid and they lost, so what?" Daelyn asked.

"He told us that their weapons *killed* them. Dead. They didn't come back."

Sean noticed more shocked expressions on the faces of the people around the table.

"Shit!" Estrella growled and smacked herself on the side of the head. "You're right! He *did* say that! And I missed it!"

"So why would that mean you have to go back?" Vincent asked.

Sean smiled lopsidedly. "Because right now only a lion can kill a djevel and not have it respawn a week later to come back again."

"But if we had those weapons, weapons that could actually *kill* them…" Maitland said.

"Well, I hate to be the one to throw ice water all over this hot idea," Chad said, speaking up, "but right now there's no way we're going through any of those small gateways. They're using them very effectively to launch harassing attacks against us to try and take pressure off the main gateway."

Sean nodded and slowly looked around the room. "I know, and that's why we need to gather supplies, weapons, explosives, and any other items we're going to need. Those attacks aren't going to last forever. The moment they slack off, we need to go through."

"We? What's this 'we' stuff?" Roxy growled.

Sean looked down at her; she did not look happy or very friendly at the moment.

"I'm going, Estrella's going."

"What!" Estrella said, looking surprised.

"Sorry, Hon. But you're the only person who knows more than I do about that place. As for who else is going…" Sean fixed Roxy with a stare that made her wilt a little, but only a little. She wasn't going to be easy to deal with on this. "That is open to negotiation. I want to take as many people as we reasonably can."

"And what happens if you get stuck in there?" Roxy growled.

Estrella nodded. "Yes, Sean. What happens? I just spent a thousand years over there; I'm not looking to do it again!"

Sean thought about that a moment.

"The sad truth is, we have to do this. There's way too many of them, and we're not cutting them down to size at all." Sean held his hand up as he saw all of his wives getting ready to argue with him. "But! But I think I may know a way to prevent getting stuck there again."

"Oh? And how would that be?" Daelyn asked, kicking him in the shin.

"Secret mystical lion shit. That's how. So I can't tell you."

Estrella gave him a look then that made it clear she had no idea what he was talking about. "It must be pretty secret if I've never heard of it."

Sean nodded. "I suspect only the First and perhaps his original pride know about it."

"And you."

Sean grinned toothily. "That's because I know magic better than any of you, so I get to figure out all sorts of mystical crap."

"You *will* talk to the First about it before you make any decisions, *right*?" Roxy growled.

Sean nodded. "Definitely. I also need to make sure my little backup plan works first. Last thing *I* want is to get stuck there either."

"Keep him honest, Estrella."

"If it's really secret stuff, the First might not want me around for it," Estrella warned.

"Tell him I said he doesn't have a choice."

"And he'll listen to that?" Estrella said with a surprised smile on her face.

Sean laughed. "Actually, he will. Roxy's already delivered on more than one threat. He knows one way or another, she'll make him pay."

Estrella sighed. "And to think I missed that."

Sean turned to their logistical heads. "Joyce? Randy? How long until we can get those lever guns?"

Randy spoke first. "They're standard rifles, so I think we could have them within a few days at most. It's the black powder ammunition that's going to be the hard part."

"I'll talk to me uncle," Daelyn said.

"I'll put together three groups," Maitland said.

"Why three?" Sean asked.

"You'll go in there with one; the other two will serve as decoys. If we can send a second group with you, we will, but we'll definitely want to send one through another gateway when it opens." Maitland smiled a little craftily then. "After all, one is suspicious. Three means we're trying to invade."

Sean nodded. "Sounds good. I gotta have a meeting with the boss," Sean said and reached down to grab Roxy's hand, "as well as the rest of my taskmasters." Grabbing Daelyn's next, he stood back up, pulling them out of their chairs.

"Come on, girls, I'm sure you're all going to want to tell me why this is a bad idea."

With that, Sean left the room as Cali, Peg, Roberta, Estrella, and Jolene followed.

After the door closed, Chad looked around the room. "You know, for the first time I *don't* envy him having all those wives."

End Book Fifteen

Afterword

Hello everyone, I'd like to start by saying, if you enjoyed this book, please go on Amazon and give me a review and a rating. I've said it before, and of course I'll say it again: Ratings are my lifeblood as an independent author, with 4- and 5-star ratings being the ones that help me the most. The more of those I get, the more likely Amazon is to show my work to other folks.

This book took a bit longer to publish, and I thought I would take a minute to tell all of you why. Originally I had decided to take a one month break to work on the next Portals of Infinity story. I was also invited by a couple of friends to join their current project. So I started working on both.

It was during this time I had a fluke accident and ruptured my left bicep. Originally I thought I'd just torn the muscle, something which will heal, but unfortunately the pain wasn't going away. Eventually I saw a surgeon, got an MRI, and then had surgery. Turns out I'd done quite a number on the arm, and healing will be a six-month process. Two of those in a very restrictive arm brace.

Added to the other things going on that I mentioned in the afterword for the last book and also on my blog, and well, April and May were very rough months. A good deal of this book was written when I was in pain. Then there was a several week break when I could barely type at all, being limited to one hand and not in much of a mood to do anything but sleep.

Things are better now. I can type, though not for long stretches yet. I'm in almost no pain at all, thankfully. Though having to adapt to being one armed and not being able to do a lot of things for the next six (well five now) months sucks. I won't be doing any motorcycle riding this summer, and I'm not allowed to cut the grass, either.

So again, I apologize for how long this took, but events took matters out of my hands.

Once again, I'd like to thank all of you for buying my books and supporting me. I do it all for you, and you all mean so much to me. Hopefully I will be able to continue to do so.

Some Recommendations: As mentioned before, I do have another name I write under: John Van Stry. If you haven't looked at it, you might appreciate my 'Portals of Infinity' series. It's currently at eight books and will continue; I will hopefully be writing the ninth book in the series within the next few months.

Some other people I enjoy reading in this genre, and you might, as well:

William D. Arand (aka Randi Darren) – Please check him out, he's good. I've been a big fan of William's since I discovered his work. It was kind of a funny moment for me when I found out he was a fan of my stuff as well. I'm honestly beginning to suspect that he can't write a bad story, because every book he writes is just so much better than the one before. I just finished 'Swing Shift', and it was great. You should really buy his books.

Blaise Corvin – The Delvers books are really a lot of fun and very much worth it. When I first came across his Delvers LLC books, I almost felt kind of jealous, because I was like 'why didn't I think of that?' I do think if you like my stuff, you'll like his as well, so check it out! And *definitely* give the

Nora Hazard book a try ('Mitigating Risk' is the first one), I'm reading it now and really enjoying it.

Michael-Scott Earle – one of these days I'm going to bribe him to finish Lion Quest.

They're all good people and great writers.

If you're into 'Harem' type fiction, you may also want to check out this group on Facebook to see who else is writing it that you might like:
https://www.facebook.com/groups/haremlit/

Again, thank you for your support and for buying my books.

My Amazon Author's webpage:

https://www.amazon.com/Jan-Stryvant/e/B06ZY7L62L/

Occasional announcements at:

https://stryvant.blogspot.com/

Jan Stryvant website at:

http://www.vanstry.net/stryvant/

(The stuff written under my real name - check it out, you might like it too!)

John Van Stry website at:

http://www.vanstry.net/

Email:

stryvant@gmail.com

Made in the USA
Middletown, DE
24 July 2019